She knew he was going to kiss her...

Her mouth was waiting for him and her eyes were already beginning to close as his lips touched hers. The kiss was hard and sweet, hungry.

'Catherine, Catherine...' Keir covered her face in burning little kisses, before taking her mouth again in a deep, long kiss that made her want more. She found herself straining into him, her hands clinging to his shoulders.

Keir was the sort of man who only happened once in a lifetime. But he had been married and widowed, and the last thing he would be looking for was serious involvement.

So...why had such a man looked at her twice?

D1461944

Helen Brooks lives in Northamptonshire and is married with three children. As she is a committed Christian, busy housewife and mother, her spare time is at a premium, but her hobbies include reading, swimming, gardening and walking her two energetic, inquisitive and very endearing young dogs. Her long-cherished aspiration to write became a reality when she put pen to paper on reaching the age of forty, and sent the result off to Mills & Boon.

Recent titles by the same author:

THE PRICE OF A WIFE
HUSBAND BY CONTRACT
SECOND MARRIAGE
SATISFACTION GUARANTEED

A MAN WORTH WAITING FOR

BY
HELEN BROOKS

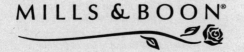

MILLS & BOON®

DID YOU PURCHASE THIS BOOK WITHOUT A COVER?

If you did, you should be aware it is **stolen property** as it was reported *unsold and destroyed* by a retailer. Neither the author nor the publisher has received any payment for this book.

All the characters in this book have no existence outside the imagination of the author, and have no relation whatsoever to anyone bearing the same name or names. They are not even distantly inspired by any individual known or unknown to the author, and all the incidents are pure invention.

All Rights Reserved including the right of reproduction in whole or in part in any form. This edition is published by arrangement with Harlequin Enterprises II B.V. The text of this publication or any part thereof may not be reproduced or transmitted in any form or by any means, electronic or mechanical, including photocopying, recording, storage in an information retrieval system, or otherwise, without the written permission of the publisher.

This book is sold subject to the condition that it shall not, by way of trade or otherwise, be lent, resold, hired out or otherwise circulated without the prior consent of the publisher in any form of binding or cover other than that in which it is published and without a similar condition including this condition being imposed on the subsequent purchaser.

MILLS & BOON and MILLS & BOON with the Rose Device are registered trademarks of the publisher.

First published in Great Britain 1998
Harlequin Mills & Boon Limited,
Eton House, 18-24 Paradise Road, Richmond, Surrey TW9 1SR

© Helen Brooks 1998

ISBN 0 263 80732 0

Set in Times Roman 10½ on 11 pt.
91-9802-57461 C1

Printed and bound in Great Britain

CHAPTER ONE

'LOOK, tell me to mind my own business if you like, but you look as though you've been in some sort of accident. Do you need help?'

Catherine heard the deep male voice but had difficulty in focusing for a moment as she raised her eyes from the hard wooden bench on which she was sitting, the big figure standing in front of her merely a dark blur. 'I…' Her voice petered out, and she tried again, taking a deep breath and trying to co-ordinate her jumbled thoughts. 'I don't know,' she whispered weakly. 'I do feel strange, but I can't remember… I'm not sure where I am.'

She wasn't making sense—she knew that—but the cotton-wool muzziness in her head and dull throbbing at the back of her eyes were overpoweringly strong.

'You must be going somewhere.' The figure crouched down in front of her, and a pair of keen stone-grey eyes held her frightened blue ones. 'This *is* your suitcase, isn't it?' He patted the big brown case at her feet as he spoke.

'Yes, but…' Again words failed her.

'Are you with anyone?'

'I don't think so.' The drumming in her head intensified as she tried to think. 'No, I'm sure I'm not, but I'll be all right,' she said as firmly as she could. 'I just need to rest a while, that's all.'

He said nothing for a moment, and then, 'You've a nasty cut on your forehead so I guess you've had a bang on the head in the not too distant past. Can you remember if you fell, or were knocked over—anything like that?'

5

'No.' She was beginning to feel frightened, the fuzzy sensation intensifying moment by moment. 'I can't remember anything,' she said a trifle desperately.

'Perhaps your name?' he suggested softly, his deep voice soothing. 'Think a minute; it will come to you.'

She stared at him helplessly as she searched in the fog of her mind, her senses registering, even in the midst of her turmoil, that he was dark and powerfully built, and handsome in a very masculine, intimidating way, with a strongly chiselled bone-structure. Thick black hair cut uncompromisingly short indicated he was a man who had little time for personal vanity, a man who knew who and what he was and exactly where he was going.

'Catherine.' She wasn't sure how she knew, but suddenly the name was there. 'My name's Catherine, and...' Just for a second something flashed across her mind, but before she could catch it it was gone. She rubbed her hand bewilderedly across her forehead and then flinched when it came away sticky and red.

'Well, Catherine, I would say you have a slight case of concussion.' He stood up as he spoke, and for a blindingly frightening moment she thought he was going to walk off and leave her.

She felt as though she had been sitting in the tiny park all her life, helplessly watching the world go by, sights and sounds registering with a strange dream-like quality before becoming merged in an overall blur that she was powerless to alter. 'Concussion?' She forced the word through the thickness in her head. 'But don't you go unconscious with that?'

'Not always.' He surveyed her with narrowed eyes, his hands thrust deep in the pockets of his jeans. 'I'm meeting my sister for lunch shortly, and I think she ought to take a look at you,' he continued firmly. 'She's a nurse so she knows what she's talking about...on medical matters,' he added drily.

'I...I don't know.' Part of her wanted to go with

him—he was the only solid thing in a world that had suddenly become an alien environment—but how did she know she could trust him? she asked herself faintly. In this day and age one didn't wander off into the unknown with a complete stranger.

'It's all right; I'm not a mad rapist or serial killer.' He seemed to know instinctively what she was thinking, and she flushed hotly at the slightly caustic note in the deep voice. 'Neither am I so desperate for female company that I would have to spirit one away against her will,' he added softly.

She could believe that at least. She gazed up at the tall, relaxed frame in front of her on which there wasn't an ounce of superfluous flesh. Oh, yes, she could certainly believe that, she thought again as the mocking, smoky-grey gaze held hers.

'Well?' He eyed her unblinkingly. 'The restaurant is just a stone's throw from here, and I've no intention of leaving you sitting here like a little waif and stray; it would spoil my lunch. I'd prefer you to walk—my carrying you kicking and screaming might damage my reputation somewhat—but either way we're going to get that head looked at. I've a nasty idea it might need a stitch or two.'

'I...I'm sure I'll be all right, thank you.' She wasn't, but she didn't know what frightened her more—the thought of going with him or the thought of him leaving her. 'I can't seem to think straight at the moment, but it will clear...won't it?' she finished somewhat pathetically.

'Come on.' He settled her indecision by the simple expedient of bending down and picking up her suitcase, before raising her firmly to her feet. 'I'm not leaving you here. Everyone has to trust someone some time, and this is your time, like it or not. My name is Keir Durrell by the way; I'm the local vet.'

What was she doing, allowing a complete stranger to

take over like this? The thought was there, but now she was on her feet it was taking all her powers of concentration just to put one foot in front of the other.

She was very aware of the height and breadth of him as he led her from the tiny square of park that was little more than a thoroughfare between the two main roads in the old Yorkshire village. Also that he had an air of command and authority that was entirely natural and very powerful—but her head was pounding unbearably now and lucid thought was not an option.

'The restaurant is just over here.' As they walked through a cobbled market place, its venerable stones ancient and warm under the hot June sun, he indicated a small square building of mellow old bricks. 'Janice should be at our table by now so you'll be quite safe.'

It was said with that same touch of dryness that had been present in his voice before, but she couldn't answer; keeping on her feet was taking everything she'd got, and waves of nausea were making the woolliness worse.

He opened the heavy, squat oak door and ushered her through, his hand at her elbow, and as he did so a tall, dark-haired girl half rose and waved in their direction from the back of the room. 'Keir? Over here.'

Catherine was overwhelmingly thankful to be able to sink into a seat, closing her eyes as she fought back the sickness. She could hear Keir at the side of her, and the general hum of lunchtime conversation and clinking of glasses, but it was remote, unreal, like a half-remembered dream in the first moments of waking.

'Catherine?' A light touch on her arm brought her eyes open, and she saw Keir's sister had moved her chair to her side. 'I think you've been involved in an accident of some kind. Would you mind if we had a look through your handbag to see if we can find a name and address or something? It might jog your memory. And I really think we ought to take you to the local hospital and get someone to have a look at your head; it's a nasty cut.'

'Here.' Catherine moved the bag off her shoulder and onto the table as the room spun. 'Please look.'

'Catherine Prentice—does that ring a bell?' Keir asked a few moments later as he fetched out an envelope from the depths of her cloth bag.

'Yes.' Catherine tried to focus on the hard male face, but it was difficult. 'Yes, that's me.' She could hear her voice from a great distance, the sound echoing in her mind.

'Okay, I think we'd better get you to a doctor right now,' Keir said grimly as she swayed in her seat. 'And stay still; I'm going to carry you.'

It was the last thing she heard before a thick, consuming darkness took over and drew her into its black void, and then she was falling, falling, the pain in her head overpowering.

'Catherine?' She could hear someone speaking her name, and struggled to respond, forcing her eyes open and then shutting them immediately as a bright light sent sharp jabs of pain stabbing through her head. 'I'm going to give you a little injection,' the voice continued in the sort of tone one normally used with very small children. 'And then you can sleep again, all right? Just relax; that's it.'

She felt a pinprick in her arm but didn't attempt to open her eyes, sinking gratefully back into the layers of darkness, and down, down, down to the peace and tranquillity of oblivion.

The next time she surfaced all was quiet and still, and as she opened tired eyes there was none of the bright light of before, just a soft and comforting semi-darkness that bathed her senses in a feeling of restfulness. She made a slight movement and immediately a figure at her side stirred, followed by the same voice as before, saying, 'You're awake, dear; that's good. Would you like a little sip of water?'

'Where…?' Her tongue seemed too big for her mouth, but she forced the words out after licking her lips. 'Where am I?'

'You're in hospital, dear.' A motherly, middle-aged face bent over her, grey hair shining in the muted light. 'You had a little bang on the head, remember?'

'Keir.'

'That's right, dear.' From the soothing note in her voice it was clear the nurse didn't have the faintest idea what she, Catherine, was talking about, Catherine thought tiredly, but she just as clearly wasn't going to challenge her on anything right now. 'Now, you shut your eyes and sleep a little more; you're over the worst now. I'm sure you'll be as right as rain in the morning. There's a bell by your hand—' Catherine felt the fingers of her right hand pressed on something hard '—so if you need anything you just ring and we'll be here straight away, all right?'

She wanted to say more, ask questions, but it was all too much effort. And as the thick blanket of sleep claimed her again she was aware of murmuring that name once more before she allowed herself to slip into the warm darkness.

'Cup of tea here for you.'

The clatter of crockery and the cheerful voice in her ear brought Catherine's eyes wide open at the same time as someone opened a blind, sending white sunlight spilling into the small room.

'Oh, thank you.' She struggled into a sitting position in the narrow hospital bed, and took the cup of tea one of the two orderlies handed her, relieved to find the terrible headache was a thing of the past. 'I must have slept the night through,' she said tentatively as the two young women smiled at her encouragingly.

'You've been asleep ever since they brought you in, love,' one of them responded buoyantly. 'Best thing for concussion. How you feelin' this mornin', then?'

'Better, much better,' she said weakly.

'That's right.' They nodded at her reassuringly.

'Had an accident, did you?' one asked brightly.

'An accident?' And then she remembered, with a rush of thankfulness that her mind was her own again. 'Yes—yes, I did. Just after I left the train station, I fell down some steps.' She stared at the two women as her mind replayed the scene. 'Someone had spilt something, and I slipped and hit my head on the edge of one of the steps,' she said slowly. 'I think I cut it.'

'You certainly did, love. Bruised yourself a bit too, I'd say. Still, all's well that ends well, eh? Lucky someone had the sense to bring you here—you could have wandered about for ages in the state you were in, and although most folks round here are okay you never know these days. Anyway, you enjoy a nice cup of tea and we'll be back with your breakfast a bit later, all right?'

'Thank you.' She smiled somewhat bemusedly, and they beamed back.

She spent the rest of the morning dozing in between having her temperature and pulse checked every half hour, and answering a whole host of questions that a brisk and very efficient sister read to her from an official-looking form.

'It's good to see you so alert,' the sister said as she stood up to leave. 'We thought it was a simple case of concussion but you seemed absolutely exhausted, which didn't help. Have you been ill recently?'

'Yes.' There was no way she was going to elaborate further, and she added quickly, 'Pneumonia. But I'm better now. I actually came to Yorkshire for a few weeks' holiday. I thought the air here would be more bracing than London's city fumes.'

'I can guarantee it.' The sister smiled approvingly.

'Well, you rest now; the doctor will be round shortly, and we'll see what he thinks of you.'

It was just after lunch when the knock sounded at her door and she sat up expectantly, thinking it was the doctor or one of his minions. But the tall, dark man who entered the room was definitely neither. 'Catherine.' It was the deep, slightly husky voice she remembered, the voice that had haunted her dreams for the last few hours. 'How are you feeling?'

'Fine.' The ugly hospital nightgown put her at a distinct disadvantage, she thought weakly, as did her pale face devoid of even a scrap of make-up, and the massive bruise that covered half of her forehead. *And he was so gorgeous.* Even yesterday, in a state of semi-consciousness, her senses had registered he was something of a hunk. But seeing him today, with mind and intellect working on full throttle, the impact of that big, lean body and devastatingly male face increased a hundredfold.

He was deeply tanned, his hair blue-black and gleaming, with a virility even the severe hairstyle couldn't diminish. And, although the handsome, classical features and hard bone-structure would demand a second glance from any female from sixteen to sixty, there was something more to him than just good looks. He had an assurance, a cool confidence that added an extra dimension to the arrogant maleness, and was powerfully attractive.

'You don't remember me?' he asked quietly. 'My name is Keir—Keir Durrell. My sister and I brought you to this hospital late yesterday morning.'

'Oh, yes, yes, I remember.' She was inexpressibly thankful he had mistaken her wide-eyed stare for confusion. She couldn't remember a time when she had ever ogled a man so blatantly, and the knowledge brought hot colour sweeping into her face. It was the knock on the head, she told herself desperately; that was what it was. She wasn't quite as well as she'd thought. 'I... Thank you—thank you so much,' she added stumblingly. 'It was very good of you—'

He swept her thanks aside with an abrupt wave of his hand. 'Anyone would have done the same,' he said dismissively. 'I just happened along, that's all. So, the memory is back, is it? That's good. The sister tells me you have a recollection of falling down some steps.'

'Yes, outside the station.' She had never felt so tongue-tied in her life, and forced a smile she hoped came across as natural before continuing, 'Silly, wasn't it? I should have been more careful—'

'What are your parents doing, letting you wander about the country on your own?'

'What?' She stared at him in amazement.

His tone had been curt, and now she was sure the dark glitter at the back of the stone-grey eyes was tightly held-in disapproval. This seemed to be confirmed when he said again, his voice cold, 'I asked you what your parents were thinking of to let you wander about alone.'

'I'm not wandering about.' Her chin rose a notch, and now the colour staining her pale, creamy skin was due to annoyance rather than embarrassment. 'And I answer to myself, no one else.'

'Do you indeed?' He came fully into the room now, walking over to the bed and looking down at her with narrowed eyes, his whole stance one of irritation and censure. 'And exactly how old are you, Miss Catherine Prentice? Fifteen, sixteen? And I want the truth, mind,' he added warningly. 'If you've run away from home now is the time to confess it.'

'If I've...?' She stared at him in absolute amazement, her anger wiping away any feeling of intimidation and putting fire in her violet-blue eyes as she hissed, 'I am twenty-one years of age. *Twenty one*, got it?'

'I don't believe you,' he said flatly, his gaze moving over the ethereal slimness of her, the fine-boned hands and pale, silvery blonde hair that framed the small face. 'You aren't a day over sixteen. Now, then, admit it.'

'I... How dare you?' All her life she had been dogged by looking far younger than her age, and normally she could take it quite well. But for him to think she was a *schoolgirl*...

Her spluttering was brought to a halt as he said, coolly and without the slightest shred of doubt, 'And a show of outrage won't wash either. If you're as old as you say you are I assume you can prove it?'

'*Prove it?*' Her voice was too high, and she lowered it a tone as he winced. 'I shouldn't have to prove it, but yes, I can,' she shot back furiously. 'Pass me my bag, would you? It's by the chair.'

'Certainly.'

He still thought she was trying to bluff him, she thought with a mixture of fury and wonder as he bent down with a lazy assurance and picked up her big, baggy cloth bag from the floor, dropping it onto the bed without a change of expression, and continuing to watch her with narrowed, hooded eyes while she rummaged about in the cavernous depths. 'Driving licence do?' she asked caustically as she fished it out from the back of her large leather purse and presented it to him with a flourish.

'Driving licence?' For the first time a touch of uncertainty showed.

'It's a document that entitles one to drive a car,' she said bitingly, 'and I've had one for nearly four years, okay?' Her headache was beginning to return, and it was all his fault! 'I'm not a runaway, or anything else you might have dreamed up,' she added tightly. 'I'm here... I'm here on holiday.' Well, she was... in a way, she told the sudden, sharp jab of conscience.

'I see.' He eyed her again after studying the driving licence. 'Then it would appear I have made a mistake; I apologise. If you would like to give me the telephone number or address of where you're staying I'll explain the circumstances of you being a day late to them, and ask them to hold your accommodation.'

'That won't be necessary.' He knew, he just *knew* she hadn't booked anything, she told herself irritably. She could see it in the hard, arrogant face and alert eyes. 'I haven't actually arranged anything yet,' she continued tightly. 'I thought I'd sort it out when I got here.'

'Did you?' It was said in the sort of patient tone one used when dealing with a recalcitrant child who was being ridiculous. 'Towerby isn't a bad size for a Yorkshire village,' he said smoothly, 'but in the middle of the holiday season, and when the weather has been good for weeks, a bed for the night isn't always on tap. However, there are plenty of other villages and towns dotted about—'

'I wanted to stay in Towerby,' she interrupted firmly. 'I'll try there first.'

'Why Towerby? One Yorkshire village is very much like another—'

'Nevertheless, I'll try there first,' she said tightly.

'Persistent little thing, aren't you?' he drawled easily, his eyes on her strained face. 'Are you always so determined?'

She shrugged warily; it hadn't been a compliment, but she was blowed if she was going to explain why Towerby was so important to her, especially to him. And she had thought she *liked* him...

'Be it on your own head.' He glanced at her hair as he spoke, its pale silveriness almost luminescent in the light from the window. 'But you could be walking the streets for hours,' he warned quietly.

'I don't care.'

She looked about twelve, sitting there in that horror of a nightie with her hair all tousled and her eyes flashing, never mind sixteen, Keir thought grimly. The urge to shake some sense into her was paramount. She was going to leave this place and tramp about Towerby looking for somewhere to stay? The girl was brain-damaged! How she'd got to twenty-one years of age was a miracle in itself.

'I'd better be going; I'm on my way to a farm the other side of Kilburn, but I had to pass here and I thought I'd call in and see how you were.' He kept his voice quite expressionless. 'I'll call by later this afternoon on my way back, if I may?'

'I might be gone by then,' she said carefully, 'but thank you again for all your help. Thank your sister for me too, would you?'

She thought she'd hit the right note of polite dismissiveness until she glanced into his face and saw the sardonic gleam in the stony eyes. 'Don't like to be told you're acting like a fool, do you?' he murmured with a calmness that was more aggravating than any show of annoyance as he walked towards the door. Once there, he turned to survey her once more, and added before she had a chance to speak, 'Goodbye, Catherine.'

And then she was alone again and calling herself every sort of name for not firing back with some cutting retort that would have put him in his place... whatever that was, she thought bitterly. She had met some arrogant, self-opinionated men in her time—London was full of them—but he took the biscuit; he really did.

Her thoughts continued to run along the same lines as she replayed their conversation over and over in her mind, getting angrier by the minute, until, when the doctor finally arrived, her cheeks were burning, her pulse racing, and her temperature was a couple of degrees above normal.

'I definitely want you here for another night of observation,' the doctor said when she asked him how soon she could leave. 'That was a nasty bang on the head, young lady, and you were pretty much out of it when you got here. I understand you're on holiday?' She nodded without speaking. 'Where are you staying?' he asked quietly.

Oh, no, not another one. She took a deep breath before saying, 'I haven't actually arranged anything yet.'

'I see.' The doctor was about thirty years older than Keir, but his face portrayed the same disapproval when he said, 'You think that was wise? I understand you don't have transport.'

'No—no, I don't,' she admitted tightly.

'And Sister tells me you've been ill recently—pneumonia. Was that all it was?' he asked intuitively.

'I don't understand what you mean,' she prevaricated quickly, flushing hotly as she stared back into the wise old eyes.

'I think you do.' His voice was gentle, but possessed of a firmness that told her he was prepared to dig for the truth. 'The concussion in itself wasn't too serious, but the way your body reacted to it suggested complete exhaustion of body and mind. Have you had some sort of a breakdown?' he asked with a directness that took her by surprise.

'I...no...yes—' She stopped abruptly. 'Not exactly,' she said after taking a deep, calming breath. 'I *was* ill for a time with pneumonia after a severe attack of flu, and then I had some bad news.' She gulped hard before she continued, 'I hadn't really recovered physically, and I found I couldn't cope too well for a time, but it wasn't as serious as a breakdown; nothing as definite as that.'

'I see.' He hadn't taken his eyes off her as she had spoken. 'Well, a holiday is probably just what the doctor ordered,' he said with a warm smile that completely belied the somewhat austere image. 'But it will have to begin tomorrow, if you are well enough to leave then. And we will have to do something about arranging accommodation, Miss Prentice. You are probably going to feel a bit shaky for a couple of days, and I really couldn't

countenance you roaming the streets looking for somewhere to stay.'

'Right.' She suddenly didn't feel like arguing. In fact
all she wanted to do was to lie back among the covers
and go to sleep.

However, once the doctor had left she found her mind
was too active for sleep, and she lay curled up in a tight
little ball under the thin sheet, staring at the tree-tops
through the window, the June sky clear and vividly blue
and devoid of even the merest wisp of a cloud.

The last few months had been hard... She closed her
eyes and drew her knees up to her waist, clasping her
legs under the thin white sheet as she lay hunched in the
bed. So hard. Why had everything happened to her? It
wasn't her fault, none of it, and yet she was the one who
felt lost, alone, abandoned. Here she was, twenty-one
years old and supposedly grown up, but she didn't know
who she was, and she certainly wasn't the person she
had thought she was all her life. And no one, *no one*
cared...

'Oh, God, help me.' It was a prayer she had whispered
almost every day over the last few months as she had
sought to draw on a power outside herself to get through.

She had always been conscious of the fact that she
was unloved and unlovable, she thought now as she
opened her eyes and stared blindly across the room. Her
parents were not demonstrative people—even with each
other—but nevertheless displayed some sort of affection
towards her brother and sister that was totally absent in
their dealings with her.

When she was younger she had occasionally made the
odd outrageous bid for their approval, but in time, as the
long, lonely years of her childhood had come and gone,
she had faced the fact that they simply did not like her.

She had wondered at times if her appearance was the
cause of their dislike—her brother and sister were tall
and dark like their parents, with brown eyes and unpre-

possessing features, and Catherine's tiny build and ethereal fairness was a stark reminder that she was different, the cuckoo in the nest.

Why hadn't they *told* her when she was a child? she asked herself for what was probably the hundredth time as the memory of that night four months ago swept in with searing clarity.

She had been working hard the preceding months, holding down a demanding job as secretary to a sales executive in a busy London office, and attending night school four evenings a week in order to obtain the further qualifications needed if she was going to advance up the career ladder. Her delight in hearing she had obtained excellent grades on the course had been dampened by a vicious attack of flu, which had resulted in complications and an admission to hospital for three weeks with pneumonia and pleurisy.

She had returned home low in both body and spirit, and with the bitter knowledge that not one of the family had visited her in hospital. If it hadn't been for the loyalty of her friends and workmates she would have been quite alone.

It was that same evening the row between herself and her mother had begun, soon to flare into a bitter exchange that had devastating consequences.

'Don't "Mother" me!' The words were spat into her white face, her mother confronting her with hands clenched into tight fists at her sides. She had bent her body at such an angle that she appeared for all the world like an enormous bird preparing to peck at the ground. 'There is no blood of mine running in your holier-than-thou veins, I can tell you. You dare to judge me because I haven't danced attendance on you the last three weeks? Why should I? *Why should I?*'

'What do you mean, there's no blood of yours in me?' Catherine had been sitting hunched over the small fire in the pristine-clean, cold little lounge, but now she rose

sharply, her eyes narrowing. Her mother continued glar-
ing at her without speaking, her sallow skin turkey-red,
and when it was apparent she wasn't going to reply
Catherine turned to her father who was standing in the
doorway. 'What does she mean?'

'Why can't you keep your big mouth shut?' Her father
flashed an angry glance at his wife before turning to
Catherine. 'Ignore her; forget it,' he muttered irritably.

'Tell her, George—go on, tell her.' Her husband's
censure seemed to tip the other woman over the edge.
'She's twenty-one in a week or so's time; she'll find out
one day so it might as well be now. Tell her what she
is, where she came from.'

'You tell her—I want nothing to do with this.' His
face was now as red as his wife's. 'I said all along it
was daft to take her on, and dafter still not to tell her.
You're the one who's always had the answers—you tell
her!' So saying, he stomped off, slamming the door violently behind him.

'You aren't our child, girl.' Her mother's voice—or
the voice of the woman she had thought of as a mother
all her life—was merciless. 'We adopted you when you
were a baby because we thought we couldn't have kids
of our own. You're my sister's child.'

'I don't believe you.' Catherine stared at the other
woman even as a tiny segment of her brain acknowledged this was the answer to the questions that had
haunted her for years. 'You've always said you have no
family, that when your parents died—'

'*I know what I said.*' The plain, middle-aged face was
pinched with spite. 'But I'm telling you now it wasn't
true, all right? When my sister was seventeen, she got
engaged to a boy who turned out to be a real bad lot.'

'She was my parents' darling, spoiled rotten from
when she was born.' The words were little more than a
snarl. 'She couldn't believe it when she got pregnant and
he upped and left her; she thought everyone would al-

ways dance to her tune.' There was a throb in her mother's voice that went far beyond maliciousness. 'After you were born she had no money and no job, and she wanted to get rid of you.'

She was enjoying this, Catherine thought numbly as she stared into the beady brown eyes; she was actually *enjoying* it.

'She was going to put you up for adoption when she was still in the hospital, so George and I decided we'd have you. It seemed like a good idea at the time.'

'Then you're my aunt?' Catherine asked dazedly. 'Is that what you're saying?'

'No, I told you, you're nothing to do with me.' The other woman sucked in her thin cheeks as she contemplated the small, pale girl in front of her, and there wasn't a shred of compassion or pity in her face or voice as she continued. 'I was adopted myself, you see, for the same reason George and I took you on. But then your mother arrived seven years later and from that moment I might as well not have existed. Everything was given to Anna—new clothes, toys—she only had to ask for something and she got it.'

'And you hated her,' Catherine said flatly, her body shrinking away from the venom in the face in front of her.

'Yes, I hated her.' She was spitting out the words now, a deep bitterness grooving the lines more markedly round her eyes and mouth. 'She was beautiful, very beautiful, something my parents never let me forget for a minute. It was all Anna this, and Anna that—'

'Then why did you help her?' Catherine asked bewilderedly. 'If you hated her so much why did you take me?'

The older woman's eyes flickered and then fell from hers as she turned and walked over to the narrow window at the far end of the room, her back stiff and straight. 'Because it suited us,' she said tightly without turning round. 'You have had a roof over your head for the last twenty-one years, haven't you? I can't see you've got anything to complain about. You're lucky—luckier than most in your position.'

Her voice rose as she turned to face Catherine, her eyes narrowed and gimlet-hard. 'That's what my parents told me,' she bit out through thin lips, 'every time they pushed me away or took Anna out without me. I had to be grateful, understand my position. Well—so do you.'

And then Catherine understood. This woman was so caught up with resentment and bitterness that she had taken her sister's baby in order to work some twisted idea of vengeance on her, to make Anna's child pay for all the misery she felt she had suffered in the past. That was why Catherine had always been brushed aside, shown no physical love or affection, ostracised in her own home.

And circumstances had played right into her adoptive mother's hands by presenting her with two children of her own. That really must have seemed like the icing on the cake, Catherine thought numbly. The whole exercise had been a cold-blooded plan of revenge. How could someone be like this? She stared at the woman she had always called mother as shock and horror kept her dumb.

'Well? Cat got your tongue?' the vicious voice continued.

'My real mother?' Catherine asked dazedly. 'Where is she?'

'I don't know and I don't care,' the other woman answered sharply. 'She moved away from London once the formalities were completed, and we've never seen her since. Good riddance to bad rubbish—'

'Where did she go?' Catherine asked again. 'I know you know; I can see it in your eyes.'

'Oh, can you, little Miss Clever-Pants?' The mockery was callous and fierce. 'Such a bright little thing, aren't you? Just like your mother. She was always top of the class at everything, always the best, but she got her comeuppance just like you'll get yours.'

'Where did she go?' Catherine persisted weakly. The malevolence was frightening.

'Yorkshire—a little place called Towerby—but that was nigh on twenty-one years ago.' The thin shoulders shrugged tauntingly. 'She'll be long since gone if I know anything about Anna.'

Catherine stumbled from the room then, her head feeling as though it would explode, and cried for hours in the questionable comfort of the tiny box-room she called her bedroom. She didn't sleep that night, the searing misery that was ripping her apart unbearable, but by the time the first tentative pink fingers of dawn were stealing across the night sky she had come to several irrevocable decisions.

As soon as she was well enough she would leave this house and never come back. And she would find her mother, her real mother. And when she did...she would ask her how she could possibly have abandoned her baby into the care of someone so cruel and twisted, so *wicked*, and she would make her listen to the life she had endured at the hands of her adoptive family.

And then... She gazed unseeingly at the charcoal-streaked sky, her eyes dry now and burningly bright. And then she would tell her that she hated her, that she would never forgive her, that as far as she was concerned she had no mother, and she would walk away without a backward glance. *She would.*

CHAPTER TWO

'IN A better mood now?'

The deep, cool voice brought her head jerking upright. She had been engrossed in her thoughts and hadn't heard the door open, but now she saw Keir framed in the doorway, his dark face unreadable. 'I wasn't... I'm not... What are you doing back here?' she asked tightly. 'I thought you'd got a farm to go to?'

'I have.' He eyed her sardonically. 'And please try to restrain your enthusiasm at my presence, it's quite embarrassing.'

The none too subtle reminder that she was being exceptionally rude brought hot colour into her cheeks, but in the next moment he stepped into the room again, speaking in a lazy, relaxed manner that nevertheless grated on her overwrought nerves.

'I thought I'd make a few enquiries regarding accommodation before I left,' he said easily. 'See if anything was available. So I phoned all the possibilities in Towerby.'

'Yes?' Say something, say you're grateful, thank him, *something*, she told herself desperately, but her mind seemed to have totally seized up.

'And there's nothing.' He came to a halt by the bed and reached out for the straight-backed chair at the side of it, hooking it with two fingers and swinging it round so that the back was against his stomach as he sat astride it, his face on a level with hers. 'Zilch.'

'Oh.' Why hadn't she brushed her hair, put on one of her own nighties from her suitcase in the corner of the room, since he'd been gone? she asked herself weakly.

She must resemble something even the cat wouldn't drag in.

'So I had a little word with Janice and we've got a proposition for you,' Keir continued smoothly. 'Something for you to think about over the next twenty-four hours.'

'Oh, yes?' Say something other than 'oh' or 'yes', please; you're not stupid, you're quite intelligent—and you certainly aren't the silly little schoolgirl he took you for either, she told herself helplessly.

'Well, in a nutshell, you're looking for a place to stay for a couple of weeks, and we happen to have a spare room that's recently been vacated by the veterinary student who's been staying with us for the past twelve months,' Keir said quietly. 'If you've really set your heart on a holiday in Towerby, it would seem the ideal solution, yes?' The grey eyes were narrowed and piercingly intent on her face. 'But think about it. You might decide somewhere else would do just as well—here in Compton, perhaps.'

'Oh, I couldn't impose—'

'Think about it.' He interrupted her hot-faced mumbling with a cool-eyed nod, his voice brisk and devoid of expression. 'The doctor tells me you're here for another twenty-four hours at least. There's no rush; the room's not going anywhere.'

'Keir—'

'And now I've really got to go.' He stood up, looking very masculine in black denim jeans and a denim shirt that was unbuttoned at the neck, showing just a smidgen of dark, curling body hair that drew her eyes like a magnet.

Help... The thought was there, but what exactly the silent cry meant she wasn't sure.

'I'll call by later, okay?' He didn't wait for an answer, walking to the door and then turning to survey her with smoky-grey eyes. 'And sleep the afternoon away; you look as though you need it.'

Charming, absolutely charming! The door had already shut as the import of his words hit home. And he thought she'd take any favours from him? She'd rather die first. She sprang out of bed as though on a spring, and then had to wait for her head to catch up with the rest of her as the room swam and dipped.

She had never met such an infuriating, arrogant know-it-all in her life, she thought caustically as she padded to the loo and back, her legs feeling as though they belonged to someone else. Not that her knowledge of men was particularly profound, she acknowledged wryly as she climbed gratefully back into bed and waited for her heart to stop pounding.

She had had the odd boyfriend since leaving school, but nothing serious. This was partly due to her parents making it clear her friends were not welcome at the house, but also because she hadn't met anyone who had remotely stirred her interest beyond platonic friendship, and her job combined with her college course had left little time for fun.

All work and no play... Was she dull? She twisted restlessly in the bed as the thought hit home. Oh, what did it matter? What did anything matter but finding her mother, the person who had betrayed her so heartlessly? All the rest was dross, nothing. She turned over, burying her face in the pillow as the tears flowed, hot and acidic.

The afternoon passed slowly, very slowly. She spent most of the time gazing out of the window at the view stretching away in front of her. The hospital was built in a wonderful position on an incline overlooking an old Yorkshire town of craggy grey stone, and with rich, swelling moorland behind it that carried the scent of a thousand summer flowers. One of the nurses had told her the hospital serviced all the villages hereabouts, including Towerby, which was some miles away over the fells.

There was a winding river in the distance, meandering its way through tranquil countryside dotted with grazing sheep, and on the far horizon what looked like the ancient remains of an old castle, crumbling now after years of relentless attack by the elements.

It was peaceful. She continued to gaze out of the window as her thoughts moved on. Peace was what she so desperately craved at the moment. Would she ever feel happy again? She shook her head slowly. Had she ever really felt happy in the first place? She couldn't remember a time when she hadn't been aware that something was missing, and that she was searching, searching for something that always just eluded her.

But now an inner certainty told her this was her time to be strong and follow the desires of her heart, wherever they led her and whatever heartache ensued. She *had* to find her mother—it wasn't a whim, it was an overwhelming conviction that seemed to come from something or someone outside herself and grew stronger every day.

She was lying in bed idly flicking through a magazine one of the orderlies had brought in when Keir returned later that evening. This time he had Janice with him.

'Hi there.' Janice bustled into the room in a flurry of starched uniform and neat black shoes, her hair pulled into a severe knot at the back of her head and her pretty face preoccupied. 'I can't stop—I'm late already and Sister'll kill me—but I just wanted to see how you are and say you're more than welcome to stay with us, you know. It'd be great to have another woman about the place, actually.'

'It's very kind of you, but I couldn't, really. It's not your fault I didn't have the sense to book something before I came.' It was easier to admit she'd been wrong to Janice, much easier. But she was aware of Keir on the perimeter of her vision as she concentrated on the other woman, and didn't dare turn her gaze on the figure leaning nonchalantly against the far wall. 'I don't want to interfere with your lives—'

'Don't be so silly; there's no question of that.'

Janice smiled sunnily, her grey eyes—which were a softer hue than her brother's—dancing as she surveyed the pale, slim girl in the bed, and her mouth turned up at the corners, revealing pearly white teeth. Catherine found herself wondering what their parents looked like to have produced two such exceptionally good-looking children, and her thoughts prompted her to say, 'But your parents—wouldn't they mind a total stranger suddenly invading their home?'

'The aged ones don't live with us,' Janice returned cheerfully. 'But I'll leave Keir to explain about that. I really must dash; I'm on nights on the men's surgical ward this week and they always keep us on our toes. Men are such babies, aren't they?'

She swung round and was out of the door while a goodbye was still on Catherine's lips. At his sister's exit Keir levered himself off the wall and walked lazily to her side, hooking the chair as he'd done before and sitting astride it before he spoke. 'Convinced?' he asked drily.

'What about?' She knew of course, but needed the time the prevarication bought.

'That the room is going begging and you're more than welcome to use it,' Keir said easily. He'd changed since lunchtime; now the tall, lean body was encased in loose grey cotton trousers and a thin charcoal shirt that made the broad shoulders seem even broader in the small white room. 'I tend to work all hours—vets do,' he added wryly. 'And Janice normally sleeps when she's not working or out with her fiancé. You could have a key and do your own thing.'

'And your parents?' she asked bemusedly, her senses registering the faint but delicious smell of aftershave and the sheer *power* of him in a way she could well have done without.

'They live down south—Cornwall to be exact; they moved there two years ago,' he said quietly. 'My mother came from Bude originally so there are still plenty of relations in that neck of the woods, and for years my father has suffered with arthritis which has been getting progressively worse. The doctor thought the milder climate would help him; the winters are pretty rough here, and very cold.'

'Has the move helped him?' she asked carefully when he paused a moment.

'On the whole, yes.' He smiled slowly and her heart stopped beating, and then raced at a furious pace at the transformation of the handsome and very male face, at the way his features mellowed and softened. 'He's still as irascible as ever. He drives my mother to distraction half the time, but they are quite devoted to each other.'

'Are they?' The words produced a dart of such painful longing that she changed the subject quickly. 'So are you and Janice in the old family home?' she asked quietly.

'No, that was sold to buy the property down south. But I had already taken on the veterinary practice in Towerby some months before when the old vet retired, and was living in the flat above the surgery premises. Janice and I decided it was logical for her to move in—she was in the midst of her training, added to which she had just decided Michael was the one for her and didn't want to leave Yorkshire.' He shrugged easily, the big shoulders bunching under the thin material.

'The flat's a decent size. It has three bedrooms and a kitchen and lounge so we're not on top of each other at all. Janice finished her training twelve months ago and secured a job here, and the practice has come on in leaps

and bounds, so there's no reason for anything to change
until she marries Michael.'

'You seem very sure of what you want.'

It was unreasonable, but his confidence and cool
self-possession grated on her. Something of what she
was feeling must have come over in her voice, because
his face was straight when he replied, 'And that's a bad
thing?'

'I didn't say that.'

'You didn't have to.' He eyed her grimly for a moment. 'You don't like me much, do you, Catherine?' he
asked in a deceptively soft voice that masked the portent
of his words for a second.

'I...that's ridiculous; I don't know you.' She knew her
face was flaming—she could feel the heat burning her
cheeks—but she had never felt so embarrassed in all her
life. He had rescued her when she was ill—behaved like
the original white knight in shining armour, if she
thought about it—and then offered her the use of a room
in his home, and all she had done was to act as though
he were the Marquis de Sade personified, she thought,
horror-stricken.

But he was right...in a way, although she wasn't sure
if she actually *disliked* him. It was more...he disturbed
her, unsettled her, she thought weakly. He was too determined, too virile, too...male.

'No, that's true, you don't know me,' he said quietly,
standing up as he spoke, and looking down at her with
that intent, perturbing directness she had noticed more
than once. 'And I've an idea you intend to keep it that
way—or are you going to accept the offer of a bed for
a few nights until you can find something else?'

Put like that it sounded so reasonable, so practical,
that she really couldn't think of a reason to refuse.
Besides which, he had made it clear that to say no would
be churlish in the extreme. But she didn't *want* to form
any link, however tenuous, with Keir Durrell, so it was

with some amazement that she heard herself saying, 'Thank you, that's very nice of you. I'll find somewhere else as soon as I can...so you can have your home back to yourselves,' she added hastily as the dark eyebrows rose sardonically.

'Of course.' His voice was very dry, and her cheeks burnt even hotter, if that was possible, as he walked over to the door and turned to survey her with that devastating grey gaze. 'I'll ring the hospital tomorrow morning and see if you are going to be able to leave,' he said quietly with very little expression in his deep voice. 'And if so I'll pop across and fetch you after morning surgery.'

'There's no need for that,' she said quickly. 'I can get a bus or a taxi; I'm used to looking after myself.'

'Nevertheless...' He opened the door and glanced across once more. 'I'll fetch you.'

'I don't want—' But he had gone, the door swinging shut behind him and cutting off her voice as she stared exasperatedly across the room, already bitterly regretting her decision, but without really knowing why.

The sun was sailing high in a cloudless blue sky when Keir arrived just after lunch the next day, striding into the quiet little hospital room with the force and energy that were an intrinsic part of the man, and dispelling the hushed hospital atmosphere as he did so.

Catherine was feeling incredibly nervous, and furious with herself for allowing her nerves to be so affected, so her smile was a little strained as she looked up from the book she had been trying to read for the last half hour.

'All ready?'

Tell him—tell him you aren't coming, that you've changed your mind, that you'll be quite happy staying somewhere other than Towerby, she told herself fiercely. She'd been rehearsing a little speech while she'd been pretending to read, but somehow, with Keir Durrell very much in the flesh in front of her, words failed her. In fact—and the knowledge was galling, incredibly gall-ing—she didn't dare.

With his earlier comments in mind, she had dressed simply but not too casually, knowing that the jeans and big baggy tops she usually favoured enhanced the im-pression of a young schoolgirl. Her tailored trousers and close-fitting waist-length blouse in soft blue were quite elegant, and with her hair in a loose knot on the top of her head and a careful application of light make-up she felt she could pass for at least eighteen, if not her true age. Anyway, she felt more in control like this, she re-minded herself firmly, and she had an idea that wouldn't be a bad thing around Keir Durrell.

'This is really very good of you.' She found she was practically trotting at his side in an effort to keep up with his long strides as they walked out of the hospital and into the hot car park. 'I'm sure I'll get something else in a few days and be out of your hair—'

'Catherine.' He stopped abruptly, putting down her suitcase and turning to take her arms in his hands as he faced her, his deep voice holding a dark quality that silenced her more effectively than any show of annoy-ance would have done. 'The room is yours while you stay in Towerby, all right? Just let it drop now.'

'I was only saying—'

'I know what you were saying, and *I* said let it drop.' She was like a wisp of thistledown in his hold, he thought as his stomach muscles tightened at the con-tact—so fragile, a breath of wind could blow her away. 'The room is there; it's ridiculous for you to pay for something else.'

'But I must pay you.' She stared at him, aghast. 'I can't possibly—'

'You can possibly.' His eyes were narrowed against the piercing white sunlight, his jet-black hair and the vivid whiteness of his shirt a startling monochrome against the different shades of green in the view spread out before them. Again something gripped her heart, causing her to jerk from his hold with more haste than finesse.

'I'm here on holiday,' she said stiffly. 'I expect to pay for my accommodation.'

'Then it can be in kind.' His voice was flat and without expression, but she knew her reaction had registered from the grimness of his face. 'The phone rings incessantly, especially in out-of-surgery hours and in the evenings; it would be a great help to have another pair of hands to answer it and take messages, especially if I've been called out already and the matter is urgent and I need notifying. And there are other little things that will become apparent. Not that any of this would be expected of you.' He let go of her now, walking over to a smart Land Rover and opening the passenger door for her to climb in. 'But if you happened to be around and could help it would be appreciated. So, quits, eh?'

'But it doesn't seem fair,' she protested once he had shut her door and joined her in the Land Rover, his big body and long legs suiting the large vehicle. 'You don't really benefit from the arrangement.'

'And you think the only reason we should do something is if we personally benefit from it?' he asked smoothly, making no effort to start the Land Rover as he turned sideways in his seat to face her, his dark face expressionless, and one arm on the back of her seat.

'No, no, of course I don't,' she said sharply. 'That's not what I meant.'

'What *did* you mean, Catherine?' The deep voice was still cool, with a thread of steel underlying the silkiness.

'Just... Oh, it doesn't matter.' She raised her head slightly and stared at him out of big violet eyes, her whole body language expressing the fact that her defences were up and remaining up.

'Have you contacted your family since you've been

in hospital? Presuming you have a family, that is.' It was straight for the jugular, and she flushed violently before tearing her eyes away from his to look out of the window. This man was too perceptive by half, she thought painfully. He knew there was something wrong and he was digging, but she'd rather die than reveal her past to him.

'No.' She thought briefly about lying, but decided she would set the record straight now; it would stop any pertinent questioning in the days ahead—hopefully. 'My family aren't interested in what I do or where I am,' she said tightly.

'You don't live with them?' he asked softly, his eyes on her pale profile as she stared through the windscreen.

'No.' The memory of that last, bitter farewell was hot and caustic in her mind; the savagery in the eyes of the woman she had called mother had been frightening as she had screamed her venom into Catherine's face. She had been living on a powder keg of hate all her life without knowing it; how could she have been so *blind*? she asked herself for the hundredth time. And the man she had known as a father had made no effort to stop his wife as she had hurled abuse at Catherine, and her brother and sister had seemed to actually enjoy the scene. And she had thought they were her *family*.

'No, I've a flat in London,' she said quietly as she dragged her mind back from the degradation and pain. 'With some friends.' She hadn't, but she balked at admitting she was homeless on top of everything else.

Anyway, it was only a half-lie, she told herself reassuringly. Some of the girls she used to work with shared a house in Kensington, and they had said she could move in with them. But she had decided on a clean break, handing in her notice and severing all ties with London, intending that once she had settled her business down here she would move somewhere quite different and start again—Manchester, perhaps, or

Birmingham—anywhere big and impersonal. She had enough money in her building society account to live quite comfortably for some months; there was no rush.

'And you don't want to let your friends know you're all right?' Keir persisted softly.

'No.' No one cares, can't you see that? she screamed at him silently. No one cared, and she was going to make sure she didn't care about anyone either in the future. If you didn't get close to anyone they couldn't hurt you—simple.

But she wouldn't be able to rest until she found out about her mother—where she was, *who* she was, why...why she hadn't been able to love her. What was the matter with her that her own mother had given her away and walked out of her life without a second thought? And, worse, given her to the person who had reason to hate her.

'Catherine?' She became aware he had spoken her name more than once, and turned her head quickly, a brittle smile on her lips. 'What's wrong?' he asked quietly.

'Nothing.' Everything. 'Shall we go?' she said brightly, turning her head to look through the windscreen again. Go—go now, she prayed tightly, before I break down and say something silly or howl like a baby.

He said nothing for a long moment, and then started the engine abruptly, his face set and cold and his mouth grim. They drove right through the old Yorkshire town without speaking a word, the atmosphere in the Land Rover taut. But when they left the houses behind, the warm June air and the beautiful scenery soothed her agitation, and she found herself saying, 'I...I do appreciate you coming to fetch me, Keir; I know you must be very busy.'

He shrugged, the movement offhand and very male, and again the sheer power in his dark masculinity rose up and caused her breath to catch in her throat and her

stomach to flutter nervously. She should never have
agreed to stay in his house, she thought desperately. It
was crazy, madness, because somehow, however she
tried to explain it away to herself, she felt threatened by
him.

She'd met handsome men before, fascinating, charis-
matic men—one often did in the big cities—but she
hadn't met anyone like Keir Durrell. And it wasn't his
darkly chiselled good looks, or the lean, honed body, or
even the authoritative self-assurance and control he exerted as naturally as breathing. It was something beyond
all that—a magnetism, an overt sexiness that scared her
half to death, much as she hated to admit it. If he wanted
a woman he would take her. Her eyes opened a little
wider at the thought, and hotness invaded her limbs as
she pictured his sensual mouth. And when he took her
it would be...wonderful.

Oh, what was she doing? She almost wriggled with
irritation and disgust, and stopped herself just in time,
sitting straight and stiff in the seat. What did she know
about the act of making love anyway? Apart from in the
odd torrid novel, that was. He could be useless in bed,
cold, impotent, even... She glanced from under her eye-
lashes at the hard, sculptured face, her gaze dropping to
the big, firm hands on the steering wheel. But she
doubted it. She certainly doubted it.

'It's not too far to Towerby.' She jumped visibly as
he spoke and hoped he hadn't noticed. 'We're going
over the fells; it's a pretty route,' he said easily, appar-
ently quite relaxed while she was turning inside out, she
thought ruefully, as nervous as a kitten. Still, men like
him didn't get hot and bothered around *schoolgirls*—his
words had rankled more than she would have liked—
and he had made it plain that was exactly how he viewed
her.

But then, as the journey unfolded, she forgot all about
her confusion and pique in her delight at the vista spread

out before them. The hot summer sun was beating down as they drove higher into the clean, pure air, the road ahead deserted as the vehicle climbed into a remote landscape where the sweet perfume of warm grass and wild flowers hung heavy and redolent in the stillness.

Rocky streams, the water crystal-clear, and enchanting miniature waterfalls seemed to appear around every corner, the wide open spaces with the great expanse of blue sky overhead captivating. For the rest of her life Catherine was to remember that journey as something set apart from real life, a breathtaking introduction to the beauty of the Yorkshire Dales.

'I was down at that farm most of the night.' As he spoke he gestured to a little doll's house far below them that was surrounded by grazing sheep—little dots of white wool on the green hillsides. 'A difficult foaling,' he continued evenly, 'but it ended well, with a whopper of a colt, and the mare forgot all her troubles the minute he was born. However many times you see it, it still continues to amaze, that fierce mother love.'

'Yes.' The pain that pierced through her was so acute she couldn't say any more. Even the creatures of the fields got it right, so why not her mother?

It was just after two o'clock when they drove into the quiet little village of Towerby, passing the thirteenth-century church and old coaching inn before pulling off the road and driving through wide-open large wooden gates into a small cobbled yard. 'We've arrived.' Keir glanced at her as the engine died, and the twittering of birds became apparent in the sluggish air. 'I'm taking you in the back way; the front is used mainly by patients and their owners.'

'Right.' He had already left the vehicle as she spoke, walking round to her side and opening her door before lifting her down onto the sun-warmed round stones.

'Welcome, Catherine.' His voice was very deep and his hands were warm around her waist as she stood in front of him, her face lifted up to his, and then, as their eyes caught and held, the moment lengthened. Her heart began to thud as he bent his head, but not to capture her lips as she had feared—*feared?*

No, the brief touch of his mouth on her forehead was the sort of chaste kiss one bestowed on maiden aunts or budding teenagers, she thought snappily as he released her immediately and walked over to a six-foot wooden fence that bordered what was clearly the end of a long terraced garden.

'Mind the cobbles.' His smile was easy and his voice cool as he turned with his hand on a small door cut into the fence. 'Don't twist your ankle. These cobbles look attractive enough, but they are renowned for keeping the local doctor busy.'

'Really?' She tried to keep all trace of testiness out of her voice, and smiled brightly as she joined him, stepping through the open door and into a long walled garden containing numerous fruit trees scattered about a thick green lawn. The high stone walls were covered in vibrant green ivy, and a narrow path wound and curled towards the house some hundred yards away, past the odd flower-bed full of gaily coloured blooms.

'It's lovely,' she breathed softly. It was. The melodious drone of busy insects was faint on the still, warm air, and a host of velvet-petalled wallflowers perfumed the air with the scents of summer. 'So peaceful.'

'Not when the surgery is in progress,' he said drily, taking her arm as he led her towards the house. She was vitally aware of his body, not least the easy animal grace with which he moved, and again she found it bothered her. Not that she wanted any attraction between them, she told herself sharply. Of course she didn't—just the opposite in fact. But he was one of those men whose masculinity couldn't be ignored, and it was…unsettling.

'We seem to have had an influx of bad-tempered cats

and dogs lately—the hot weather getting to them, no doubt—and it sounds like a circus most days.'

She nodded, but didn't answer. This *was* peaceful, whatever he said. No harsh words, no snide comments, no poisoned little darts to wound and smart. Animals she could take; it was human beings she had trouble with.

They entered the house through a heavy oak door, and she found herself in what appeared to be a long, narrow corridor, the floor stone-flagged and the walls painted white. 'Come and have a look around before surgery,' Keir invited. 'Meet a few of the patients. You do like animals, I take it?' He clearly didn't consider it a possibility she might not.

'Very much so,' she said at once.

'I thought as much.' His voice was warm and satisfied.

'What would you have done if I'd said I didn't?' she asked curiously, glancing up into his dark face as she spoke.

'Changed your mind.'

She felt the arrogance in the statement was typical of him, and frowned quizzically. 'And if you couldn't?' she persisted, determined not to let it go. 'What then?'

'I always do what I set out to do.' He eyed her mockingly. 'If I want something bad enough I don't take no for an answer, however long it takes.'

The caustic reply that sprang to her lips never had the chance to be voiced, which was probably just as well, because in the next moment he opened the nearest door and pushed her through ahead of him. 'This is the recovery room,' he said quietly, 'complete with residents.' He indicated the stack of blanket-lined cages that dominated two walls, several containing sleepy patients who eyed them dozily. 'The room's wired so that we can hear any sound from here all over the building if so required.'

'Are any of them very ill?' An engaging little puppy

occupied one cage, and she gestured at the small dog who had one leg encased in plaster. 'Him, for example?'

'He'll be fine.' Keir drew her out of the room and back into the corridor as he spoke. 'Although his owner's purse will be a good deal lighter in the process. He was left alone with a couple of older dogs who decided they'd use him in a tug-of-war contest. Fortunately the owner heard his squeals and rescued him before too much damage was done, but the case is typical of owners who don't understand animal behaviour. The lady was visiting a friend and thought it would be nice for her puppy to get to know the other dogs, so they shoved them all in a room together and went off to the kitchen to have coffee.'

His tone was scathing, and Catherine felt a moment's sympathy for the unfortunate owner; she had a feeling Keir wouldn't mince words in such a situation.

'Here's my operating theatre.' He opened another door a little further on, and she saw a clinically clean white-washed room with all the necessary equipment and paraphernalia associated with a hospital theatre.

'The surgery kitchen.' He opened yet another door. This room too was immaculate, and smelt faintly of anti-septic and carbolic. 'Used mainly for preparing the animals' meals and so on. Some of them are on very special diets, and the preparation can take some time.'

This was more than just a promising career to him. She glanced at the hard, dark face from under her eye-lashes as he led her to the end of the passage. The fervent note in his voice, his pride in his little empire...this was his life's blood. He really *cared* about the animals, she thought wonderingly, with a force of emotion she wouldn't have thought this self-assured, somewhat for-midable man capable of.

As they left the passageway the area widened into a large square hall, with black and white tiles on the floor and the front door directly before them. Keir gestured to a room on the right. 'The main waiting room with the reception area. There are three consulting rooms beyond that,' he said briefly, 'and also a storeroom. As you can imagine, our patients range from the big beasts on the farms right down to pet hamsters, so we cover a vast range of animal life.'

'I can imagine,' she agreed meekly.

'And—' He stopped abruptly, turning to glance down at her suspiciously from his considerable height. 'Are you laughing at me?' he asked slowly.

'No.' And she wasn't, not really—in fact his enthusiasm made her feel anything but amused, generating as it did a reluctant tenderness at his vulnerability that she could well have done without.

'Good.' The grey-eyed gaze held hers for one moment more before he turned to the left, his hand on a door beyond which muffled whines had been steadily building as they had been talking. 'And now you'd better meet Muffin and the gang—brace yourself,' he warned just a second before the door opened and a flood of animals surged into the hall, to the accompaniment of high, joyous barking and deep, throaty woofs.

'Are they all yours?' She had crouched down on her haunches to say hello to the dogs, which ranged from the biggest, most powerful long-haired German shepherd she had ever seen to a tiny, diminutive Yorkshire terrier who kept leaping into the air as though on invisible springs. 'How many are there?'

'Yes, they're all mine, and there's six of them.' He spoke a sharp word of command and the pack melted into an ingratiating circle at his feet, tails wagging frantically. 'This is Muffin, the indisputable boss,' he continued quietly, patting a soulful-eyed cocker spaniel. 'She was my mother's dog originally, but my mother decided she couldn't separate her from the others when she went to Cornwall.

'Sally, her best friend and ally—' he gestured to the

Yorkshire terrier '—and James and Josh. They are cross-bred beagles my father found abandoned in a disused caravan some years ago. Megan is a whippet who was used as a breeding machine until we got hold of her, and the German shepherd is the youngest of the lot. I've had him from a pup, and he's two now. He was an indulgence, considering we'd already got five dogs in residence, but I'd always promised myself a long-haired German shepherd.'

'He's magnificent.' She eyed the powerful dog warily.

'He's the softest of the lot,' Keir said ruefully. 'They all boss him about, especially the little Yorkie.'

All this love. She stared at him for a moment as something gripped her heart so tightly it hurt, and it was her inner turmoil that caused her voice to be sharp as she said, 'I always thought vets had a rule not to become involved with their patients, and certainly not to take in waifs and strays.'

'Did you?' His voice was cool, almost expressionless. 'Then perhaps you've been involved with the wrong sort of vets.'

'I haven't known any,' she returned indignantly.

'Then how could you possibly make a statement like the one you just did?' he countered evenly.

'I...I've read books, articles, that sort of thing,' she admitted in feeble defence of her criticism.

'Ah, I see.' The dark face told her more eloquently than words exactly what he thought of her reading material. 'I always prefer my opinions to be made first-hand,' he continued drily. 'That way I've no one but myself to blame when I fall flat on my face.'

She felt her colour flare at the none too subtle rebuke, and the defence mechanism she had employed for years to deal with jibes from her family sprang immediately into place. 'I'm sure you never fall flat on your face,' she said with a honeyed sweetness that curled at the edges with biting sarcasm. 'You know so much about everything, you're so wise.'

'Thank you.' He bowed slightly, his eyes infuriatingly amused at her attack. 'That's the nicest thing anyone has ever said to me.'

'Oh, I can't believe that.' She heard herself continue with a feeling of dismay, but somehow she couldn't stop, couldn't betray any vulnerability in front of this big, arrogant, *together* individual. 'Girlfriends, for example— they must have been complimentary now and again?' She smiled brightly. 'Assuming you've had girlfriends, of course,' she added sweetly, bending to fuss one of the dogs as she spoke.

'Not recently.' If she had been looking at him she would have noticed the change in his face.

'Oh, but—'

He stopped her blundering on any further with a touch on her arm, his face closed and expressionless as he said, his voice quiet, 'My wife died just over eighteen months ago; she had a degenerative blood condition that was incurable. I haven't dated anyone since.'

'Oh...' She straightened slowly, her eyes wide with horror. 'I didn't know—I'm sorry, I'm so sorry... I...I don't know what to say.'

He had been married—*married*? But, of course, she might have known a man like Keir Durrell wouldn't have remained single so long, that he would have been snapped up. And his wife had died...

'There was no reason you should know.' His voice was cool, remote, and as he ushered the dogs back into the room she stood quite still, her mind racing. Of course there was no reason she should have known, she told herself painfully. No reason at all. She was here for two or three weeks, that was all, and only because he considered her a waif and stray in much the same way he did the animals he took under his wing.

He had extended a hand of condolence, pity, shown

charity to someone he clearly considered young and foolish and incapable of looking after herself—and it was nice of him, very nice. She realised she was wringing her hands together, and unclasped them abruptly. Very nice...

CHAPTER THREE

'COME and meet Sandra, my receptionist, and then I'll take you upstairs to the flat and show you your room.'

She brought her head, which had been drooping forward, sharply upright as Keir turned from shutting the door. As he saw the look on her face he stopped abruptly, his smoky gaze holding hers.

'I'm sorry, Keir.' She had to say it now, properly, before she lost her nerve. 'About your wife—what I said—'

'Catherine—'

'No, please listen.' She took a deep breath, her hands clasping again without her being aware of it, although the big, dark man looking down at her was aware of every movement she made. 'I... You've been so kind, helping me and then offering me a place to stay, and it's just that—' Oh, how did you explain the unexplainable? 'I'm not used to people being kind,' she murmured helplessly. 'I know I'm prickly—'

'Hedgehogs have the sweetest faces.' His voice was like thick silk, and held a note that made her nerves quiver. 'Have you ever noticed that?'

'Hedgehogs?' For a moment the metaphor didn't register, and then she blushed furiously.

'And it's all right—really.' It wasn't, but she felt her tension and confusion drawing him up and away from her as he recognised her distress. 'Forget it.'

'Forget it?' It was like a slap round the face. Did he really think she was so shallow that she could push to one side the pain and grief that must have accompanied his statement 'My wife died eighteen months ago'? Did he think she was so wrapped up in herself that she couldn't recognise another's agony? 'I can't, and I am grateful—'

'I don't want you to be grateful.' The silk had been torn aside and there was steel underneath for just a second before he said, 'That's not necessary, Catherine. Just enjoy your holiday, okay?'

'Keir—' Her mouth was open to say more, to tell him that this was not a holiday, that it was a mission, a mission to find someone who didn't want to be found, someone who had betrayed her, cast her aside. But then the door to the reception area opened and the moment was lost.

'I thought I heard voices.' The girl was pretty, very pretty, with a heart-shaped face and big green eyes, her luxuriant hair the sort of ash-blonde colour that owed its attractiveness to a bottle but was none the less stunning for it. 'I was just checking everything was all right.'

'Thanks, Sandra.' Keir's voice was easy now, warm even, and Catherine could see why. Sandra had the sort of looks and figure most models would be proud of. 'I was just bringing Catherine to meet you, as it happens—you remember I said she'd be staying in the flat for a while?'

'Yes, I remember.' The green eyes were as clear and cold as glass as they met Catherine's although the rosebud mouth smiled prettily. 'How do you do, Catherine? Fully recovered from your little accident?'

She made it sound as though she were a child who had fallen down and cut her knees, Catherine thought uncomfortably as she forced herself to smile and take the proffered hand. 'Yes, thank you. I feel fine now,' she said as naturally as she could, although there was something in the other girl's gaze that made her feel awkward. 'I'm just sorry to have caused such a fuss.'

'Yes...' The word could have been one of sympathy for her predicament, but somehow Catherine didn't think so. 'Keir?' Sandra's face mellowed and softened as she turned to him. 'I'm afraid there's a list of calls for this afternoon, including one at Beck's Farm; that cow still isn't feeding her calf and it's been a few hours.'

Keir nodded slowly. 'We've had trouble with that particular cow before, but an injection will set her to rights. Once she gets going she's a good little mother. I'll just check my bag while you finish showing Catherine around, okay?' His gaze swung to Catherine. 'And then I'll take you up to the flat and you can take it easy for a bit,' he added absently, although it was clear his mind was already at Beck's Farm with the cow and her calf.

'Come on through.' Sandra dragged her eyes from Keir's departing back with obvious effort, turning to walk back into the reception area without waiting to see if Catherine followed, and talking in a flat monotone as she showed her the consulting rooms and dispensary.

'So...' As they returned to the waiting room Sandra's eyes flicked over Catherine's face, and again she felt their chill in the little shiver her nerves gave. 'How long are you staying in Towerby, Catherine?'

'I'm not sure,' she said quietly. 'I don't want to impose on Keir and Janice; they've already been so good.'

'Oh, Keir's a great one for picking up strays.' Sandra laughed lightly, but the sound wasn't pleasant. 'I'm talking about animals, of course,' she added mockingly as Catherine's face straightened. 'He's a target for every lame dog in the county.'

'Is he?' Catherine stared hard at the other girl's scornful face. She had lived with dislike long enough to recognise it instantly.

'His work is his life, of course.' Sandra's eyes had narrowed on Catherine's face. 'Especially after the tragedy with Marion.'

'His wife, yes, he told me.' Thank you, thank you, *thank you* that I didn't have to ask what she was talking about, Catherine prayed silently; Sandra would have loved that. 'It must have been a terrible time for him—for everyone.'

'Yes, it was.' Sandra flicked a long lock of hair off her shoulder as she spoke, but her gaze remained locked on Catherine's face. 'I was a close friend of Marion; that's partly why I took the job when she became ill. She was Keir's receptionist too, you see. Do you work?' she asked abruptly.

The manner of asking, rather than the question, was undeniably impertinent, but Catherine forced herself not to overreact to the other girl's antagonism. She was Keir's receptionist when all was said and done, and any unpleasantness between them might be picked up by him. Besides which, she didn't want to make an enemy in her first few minutes in his home.

'I'm between jobs at the moment,' she said carefully. 'And as I'd got some money put by it seemed a good idea to take my holiday just now and have a good break before I look for something else.'

'Why the Yorkshire Dales?' Sandra managed to suggest anywhere else would have been a better idea.

'Why not?' Catherine countered lightly.

'Well, there's no nightlife for a start,' Sandra said tightly. 'And coming from London I'm sure you know how to have a good time,' she added with biting intent.

Whatever had she said or done to incur such wrath? Catherine paused a moment before she said, 'I do like to have a good time, and that's exactly what I intend to have here—plenty of long walks in the fresh air, peace and quiet, and some time to please myself.'

'Oh.' Her definition of a good time clearly didn't sit well with Keir's receptionist. 'So you're a country girl at heart?' Sandra asked flatly. 'Is that what you're saying?'

'I suppose so, but—' Catherine's reply was cut short as Keir reappeared, his dark face preoccupied, and

Sandra turned away from her to smile a smile of sickly sweetness at him which he didn't appear to notice.

'Ready?' he asked Catherine, before glancing at Sandra and handing her a sheaf of papers. 'Type those onto the surgery records, would you?' he asked absently. 'And I'll be back about four, okay? You've got the list of visits in case you need to make contact before then, haven't you?'

He didn't wait for a reply before taking Catherine's arm and ushering her firmly into the hall and up the stairs situated to one side of the front door, stopping on a large, uncarpeted landing and gesturing with his head to the stairs that continued upwards. 'Just attics and spiders up there,' he said shortly, 'along with the junk of several vets from over countless years.' He opened the heavy oak door in front of them with a key which he then handed to Catherine. 'This is yours, incidentally. If you lose it there's a spare for emergencies hanging up in the dispensary by the window. Come and go as you please.'

'Oh, right.' The speed with which he was dealing with her tied her tongue.

'Your room is the one at the far end of the hall, but explore where you like,' he said as he drew her into the flat and pointed to the end of the passageway. 'I really must go, but help yourself to food or coffee or whatever.'

'Yes, thank you.' Her voice was cautious, quiet.

He caught sight of her somewhat guarded expression just as he turned to go, and stopped, swinging round to face her again and looking down at her with narrowed, unreadable eyes. 'Don't look so scared,' he said softly. 'You might be in the wolf's lair, but he can be quite civilised when he feels like it.'

'What?'

'You weren't imagining I was going to leap on you at the first opportunity?' he queried drily.

How could he say such a thing? She was mortified. 'No, of *course* not.'

'No?' He clearly didn't believe her, and her embarrassment grew in a hot flood that stained her face and neck deep pink.

'No—I've told you,' she stammered desperately. 'I didn't think... I don't...'

'Then why are you so nervous around me, so defensive?'

'I'm not.' Oh, this was awful—*awful*.

'I think you are.' His voice was soft, gentle even, but its silkiness was embracing steel. 'Have you been hurt by a man, Catherine? Abused, perhaps?'

'No!' Her voice was too high, and she tried to moderate it as she said, 'I haven't—really.' Not in the way you mean, and not by a man, she added silently. Perhaps that would have been easier to come to terms with than having to accept that the people she had thought of as her family for twenty-one years were strangers, that they had never wanted or loved her, that her whole *life* was a lie.

'Okay, okay.' The relief that filled him was knee-trembling in its intensity. But there was something—he knew it—something that was eating her up inside. If it wasn't a man, then what the hell was it?

'You...you said you had to go,' she said shakily.

'I'm going.'

Catherine wasn't aware of the pain that had turned her violet eyes almost black; she just knew this conversation had to stop. He was being kind; she was another of his stray lambs, wasn't she? As Sandra had so pointedly made clear, he felt sorry for her. 'I...I hope you find the cow well.'

She saw him suddenly bite his lip. A husky, strangled sound escaped from his throat, and it was a moment or two before he said, with a careful lack of expression that

spoke its own story, 'I'm not going to have tea with her,
Catherine.'

He was laughing at her! She stiffened, her outrage
evident in every line of her body, but in the next moment
he leant forward to touch her face gently with the palm
of his hand in a gesture she was sure was meant to be
just comforting, but which she found...disturbing.
Especially as his nearness forced her to acknowledge the
faint, male smell of him, the broadness of his chest, the
way the sprinkling of silky black body hair revealed by
his open shirt collar suggested a hairiness that was positively threatening.

'Relax.' He had noticed her physical withdrawal at
his closeness; she could see it in the sudden tightening
of his mouth and the narrowing of his eyes. 'Like I said,
I can be quite civilised when I feel like it.'

She didn't doubt it, but what he didn't realise was that
it was not *his* control she was worried about. For some
reason her hormones seemed determined to go haywire
around Keir Durrell. She didn't want it, she certainly
didn't *like* it, but she had to face the fact that he exerted
a sexual attraction he was quite unaware of and which
was as powerful as a nuclear bomb—relatively speaking,
of course, she qualified with a touch of self-derision at
the analogy. It was making her jumpy, ridiculously so,
and it had to stop.

She took a deep breath, raised her chin and forced a
smile. 'Shall I come back with you to the Land Rover
for my suitcase?' she asked brightly, deciding it was
better not to continue a conversation in which she was
totally out of her depth. 'Then you can shoot straight
off—'

'It's already in your room; I brought it in when you
were talking to Sandra.' He stepped out of the flat as he
spoke, pausing on the square sunlit landing to say,
'Janice is still asleep, but she'll be up soon; she'll want
to have a shower and something to eat before she leaves

for the hospital. Her room is the one next to yours, incidentally.'

'Right.' She was fiercely grateful that there would be more than one thin wall separating them, which again was quite absurd but nevertheless how she felt. Somehow the thought of perhaps being able to hear him moving about, preparing for sleep, getting *into* bed, was shattering, humiliating as it was to admit it to herself. It didn't help to acknowledge that she was behaving just like the giddy schoolgirl he had taken her for either, or that her imagination seemed to run riot round this man. Oh, *why* had she accepted his offer of a room? She hadn't wanted to.

She was still pondering the thought when she realised he was halfway down the stairs and she hadn't returned his somewhat cool farewell.

The flat was surprisingly large, bright and airy, with a magnificent view over the surrounding village from the large picture window in the lounge. The small kitchen was compact and sparkling clean, with every modern appliance known to man squeezed in its tiny frame, and she was entranced to find a huge cast-iron bath in the gleaming bathroom with quaint bow legs and ball-and-claw feet. But it was when she opened the door to the room that would be hers that she really fell in love with the place.

The room wasn't large by normal standards—although compared to the tiny box-room that had been her bedroom for twenty-one years it was enormous—but it was the huge window that took up most of the far wall, and the view beyond, that made it utterly enchanting.

She stepped across the sunlit room, the colour scheme of pale lemon carpet and walls and ivory furnishings and curtains reflecting every scrap of sunshine, and leant out of the window, reflecting that it seemed as though half of Yorkshire was spread out before her. 'Beautiful...'

She breathed in the sweet, moist air for a few heady moments. 'Just beautiful.'

From her eyrie she gazed out over distant green fields of grazing sheep, the smaller bodies of still young lambs running to their mothers now and again, and gazed still further to a sweeping crescent of tree-covered hillside that rose up and up into the endless blue of the sky.

She could smell myriad scents on the warm June air, her nostrils teased by the intoxicating fragrance of flower-dotted hillsides, newly cut grass and the pulse of summer as she drank her fill of the vista. To think that people lived and worked in such surroundings every day—people like Keir...

The name broke her tranquillity and she turned abruptly, glancing across at the big suitcase on the bed.

What would he say if he found out she was up in his part of the world to confront a woman she had never seen, a woman who most definitely would not want to see her, a woman who had ignored her existence for twenty-one years? she asked herself agitatedly. Mind you, she had no reason to think her mother was still living in these parts. The reminder was one she had given herself over and over again in the last few weeks, but somehow it didn't bear weight with the conviction deep inside that her mother *was* here. She didn't know how she knew, she just did—or perhaps it was merely wishful thinking?

'Oh!' The exclamation was angry and sharp. She had to stop this perpetual cross-examination when she was alone; it was driving her mad.

She would unpack, and then just lie down on the bed for a few minutes until she heard Janice stir. It was amazing how tired she felt, considering she had been lying in bed for two days...

She awoke to a room filled with the mellow, soft shadows of dusk, the heat of the day having settled into a mild, balmy warmth that was gentle on her skin. She lay cocooned in a relaxation of mind and body that she hadn't felt in years, just watching the sky turn darker outside the window, the accompaniment of quiet baaing of sheep in the distance and the odd night sound from the village soothing.

She could be happy here. The thought was there before she had time to deflect it, and it brought her abruptly from the bed. At almost the same moment she heard Keir's deep voice rumble somewhere outside the room, Janice's softer tones less distinguishable. Her heart fluttered and raced, and she made a sound of annoyance in her throat at her weakness.

Keir wasn't in the least interested in her, and that was good—*it was*. She was going to have to concentrate all her time and energy on discreet and very careful enquiries about a woman who had moved to these parts twenty-one years ago, and the odds were heavily stacked against her succeeding, too. Romantic complications she didn't need. If her quest was fruitful she would certainly have to leave Yorkshire immediately after seeing her mother; anything else would be too embarrassing and difficult for everyone concerned. If it wasn't, then she would have to leave anyway, to continue the search. Either way, Yorkshire was closed to her.

She ignored the jolt her heart gave, and walked across to the small dressing table, sitting down and brushing out her hair so the silky, silvery waves hung free about her shoulders. Then she carefully removed every scrap of make-up so that her face had a shiny, freshly scrubbed look and contemplated her reflection in the mirror for a moment. Yes, she did look about sixteen, she reflected flatly, but that was all to the good, considering her mission.

And Keir? a quiet little voice in her head questioned slyly. What about him thinking you look young, gauche and unpolished?

A gentle knock at the door interrupted her thoughts, bringing her head swinging round as she called, 'Come in.'

'Hi.' Janice was already dressed for work as she came into the room, carrying a cup of tea. 'You've slept the afternoon away, which is exactly what I'd have prescribed.' She grinned cheerily. 'Keir's preparing the dinner, but I'd go and keep an eye on him if you don't want to be poisoned.'

'Aren't you eating?' Catherine asked anxiously, the fluttering returning tenfold at the thought of a cosy dinner for two with Keir as she accepted the cup of tea with a smile of thanks.

'Nope, I've had a sandwich, and that's all I can take when I'm on nights.' Janice grimaced, her nose wrinkling. 'It plays havoc with my digestive system. I've got to dash; Michael is on nights too, so he's picking me up in a couple of minutes.'

'He works at the hospital?' Catherine asked interestedly, putting the disconcerting matter of dinner with Keir to one side for a moment.

'He's a doctor.' Janice's face glowed. 'But that's not where we met, if that's what you're thinking. I've known him for years—all my life really.' The sound of a car horn brought the conversation to a close as Janice swung round with a quick, 'That's him; must dash,' and left the room in the same pell-mell fashion that Catherine was beginning to learn was characteristic of Keir's sister. They might be alike in looks, but that was all. Janice had none of Keir's cool authority and formidable, almost cold control.

'Feeling better? You looked all in earlier.' The quiet voice issued from the door to the kitchen as she walked through the hall after drinking the tea and changing her crumpled clothes for comfortable old jeans and a long, baggy top. The earlier resolution to look grown-up and sophisticated had gone, washed away by a heavy dose

of common sense that told her she wouldn't be able to
keep it up. She was what she was.

'Yes, thank you.' She paused in the doorway, her
senses receiving the usual jolt at the sight of him. He
was standing at the small, compact breakfast bar busily
slicing mushrooms, a tea-towel tucked into the waistband of his black denim jeans and the sleeves of his
shirt rolled up to reveal muscled, sinewy arms covered
liberally with short black hairs. The contrast of domestic
familiarity and sheer sex appeal was heady, and she felt
her toes curl.

'Good.' He looked up briefly, the devastating grey
eyes taking the whole of her in before they dropped to
the task in hand. 'I hope stir-fried chicken and salad is
okay with you?' he said easily. 'My culinary skills are
somewhat limited.'

'Yes, but I ought to be doing that; I mean—'

'Don't tell me you are one of those rare females who
feel a woman's place is in the kitchen?' he asked mockingly. 'That really would be too good to be true.'

'No.' It was a snap, born out of the agitation and
unease she always felt around this man, but she qualified
the sharpness by quickly saying, 'I just meant that in
view of everything that's happened the least I can do is
cook dinner.'

'What's happened?' He shrugged nonchalantly, the
movement bringing her eyes to the dark shadow under
the thin material of the shirt which spoke of thick body
hair, and doing nothing to lessen her nervousness.
'We've a spare room and you need a place to stay for a
while,' he said with magnificent simplicity. 'Nothing
could be more straightforward. Here, pour us both a
glass of wine if you insist on being useful; it's open.'

In her haste to obey she spilt a little of the deep red
liquid, but he didn't appear to notice, taking the glass
she offered with a word of thanks as he continued to stir
the delicious mixture in the huge wok.

Now she was actually in the kitchen it seemed rude to leave, and so she perched on one of the two long-legged stools at the end of the breakfast bar, acutely aware that the limited space brought him uncomfortably close with every movement he made.

'Tell me a bit about yourself.' It was casual, easy, but it was what she had been dreading, and for a second her thought processes froze.

'There's nothing much to tell.' The wine was mellow, fruity, and she took a big gulp before she continued, 'I was born and raised in London, I'm twenty-one years old—' he acknowledged the statement with a wry lifting of his thick brows which told her he hadn't forgotten their earlier conversation '—and I'm up here on holiday, that's all.'

'That's all?' His mouth twisted in cool disbelief. 'What about family, friends, your job?' he asked softly. 'The things that make up real life?' He turned to face her, his eyes penetrating.

Right, you knew it was coming, so just deal with this with an economy of truth, she told herself firmly. Just enough to satisfy that razor-sharp mind. 'Family consists of my parents and a brother and sister,' she said flatly. 'And—'

'Hey, hang on, hang on.' He reached out and touched her arm, and she felt the light contact in every nerve and sinew. 'Do you see much of them? Are your brother and sister older or younger than you—?'

'Younger.' She cut him short before he could ask more. 'Quite a few years younger, but there's only a year between them so they argue like cat and dog. My parents—' she took a deep breath and prayed for control '—are not like me—' thank you God, *thank you God* '—and we've never really got on.'

'I see.'

He didn't, but she didn't give him a chance to ask more. 'Friends are numerous, job is secretarial, and I think the stir-fry is burning,' she finished, still in the same matter-of-fact tone.

It took a moment for her words to register, and then he leapt to the wok, salvaging their dinner before any harm was done, while she blessed the fact that her guardian angel had been on the ball after all.

Soon after, they ate together—Catherine taut with a nervous energy that kept her from appreciating the food—at the old wooden table in one corner of the lounge, the big windows open to the scented night air, and the village lights beginning to twinkle on, one by one, as night drew a dark mantle over the world outside.

Keir chatted easily as they ate, but although his voice was calm and his manner relaxed Catherine felt the curiosity he hadn't voiced, and knew that sharp, agile brain was ticking away on quite a different level as he kept her entertained with amusing stories about his work. But as long as he didn't *ask* her it would be all right, she told herself tightly. And if he did she would have to prevaricate about her past life; there was no other way.

'Apple pie and cream okay?' He stood up as he spoke and reached across for her empty plate, the movement causing her nostrils to flare as the faint, tangy smell of his aftershave touched her senses for a fleeting second.

'Could I just have coffee?' she asked quietly.

'No.' Her eyes sprang to his dark face, and she saw his mouth quirk at her expression of surprise. 'You're far too thin; you need feeding up,' he stated firmly. 'If you don't like apple pie there's chocolate-chip ice cream or fruit cake.'

'I don't want anything.' She had stiffened at the criticism, and her cheeks were burning. 'Thank you,' she added a few seconds later, forcing the words out through gritted teeth.

'Not that you aren't lovely the way you are,' he continued as though she hadn't spoken, his eyes considering as they moved over her frame and his voice thoughtful, almost analytical. 'But you definitely need a few extra pounds.'

'Now look here—'

'So which is it to be?'

'*Keir*—'

'Two apple pies?' His voice was still quiet, but exerted a force of will she really didn't feel up to challenging.

'Oh, all right,' she muttered ungraciously. 'If you insist.'

'I do.' His voice was soft now, dark. 'I told you before I don't take no for an answer if I want something, didn't I?' he said gravely. 'And...' He paused for a moment, bringing her eyes to his. 'My profession helps me to recognise when someone's been unwell, and you've been unwell.'

It was a statement, not a question, but she nodded anyway. 'Not that I was a two-ton Tessie before that,' she said acidly, still smarting from his fault-finding. 'Not every girl has huge—' She stopped abruptly at the raised eyebrows. 'Is curvaceous,' she finished weakly.

'Who said anything about curvaceous?' he said mildly. She had the sort of beauty any red-blooded man would take a second look at, and yet the inferiority complex was as big as a house. What the hell had gone on in her life to make her so nervous, so wary? Who had bruised that delicate ego so badly that she was like a cat on a hot tin roof most of the time? He felt his stomach muscles contract as darker possibilities flashed hotly through his mind for one caustic second before he thrust them away.

No, she was an innocent; he'd bet his life on it. He'd seen too many of the other sort in his life to doubt the naive artlessness which in itself was unwittingly seductive. But nothing about her present situation added up. Girls like her didn't holiday by themselves, or if they did it wasn't in a small village in Yorkshire.

Catherine was standing at the window when he re-turned with two plates of steaming pie, her back to the door, but she turned quickly, almost guiltily, at his en-trance. 'I...I was just looking down at the village,' she said jerkily. 'It's not very big, is it? Everyone must know everyone else very well.'

'Must they?' His voice was bland, uninterested, as she scuttled back to the table, but if she had been looking at his face she would have seen the keen dark eyes were focused and intent. 'Is that good or bad?'

'Neither, just a fact.' He had moved her chair away for her to sit down again, and now pushed it under her jean-clad bottom as she sat down.

Nice bottom, he thought appreciatively—tight and rounded, and just the right span for a man's hands to cup...

'Was your wife from these parts?' She acknowledged far too late that she'd said it partly as protection against the intimacy of their meal for two, but also because she really wanted to hear about her. But once the words were out she was aghast at her tactlessness. 'Oh, I'm sorry, I shouldn't have asked; I didn't—'

He stopped the torrent of words with a cool but un-revealing voice as he said, 'Why not? Marion was not a local girl, as it happens. In fact she came from London, like you, initially. We met at veterinary college.'

She watched him as he returned to his own seat, sit-ting down and proceeding to eat a mouthful of pie before he spoke again. 'And you? Any broken hearts pining at your absence?'

'Me?' To her chagrin she blushed hotly at the per-fectly acceptable question. 'No, no, there's not.'

'Right.' There was an inflexion in his voice, just something that made her glance into the dark face searchingly, but the hard, male features were remote, implacable, as he stared back at her.

She shouldn't have agreed to stay here. Again the

thought sprang to mind, but this time it was strong and fierce and possessed of an urgency that made her nerves quiver. She couldn't begin to work him out—he made the word 'enigma' sound positively commonplace—but one thing she was sure of: *she should never have agreed to stay.*

CHAPTER FOUR

CATHERINE slept deeply that night, only once waking
briefly at the sound of a telephone ringing somewhere,
followed a few minutes later by a creaking door, footsteps and then the front door closing. She glanced sleepi-
ly at her tiny alarm clock on the side of the bedside
cabinet. Two o'clock in the morning; it had to be a night
call for Keir, she thought, moments before she snuggled
down under the covers again and fell immediately
asleep.

The next time she opened her eyes it was to a room
full of early morning sunlight, and although it was only
six o'clock she found it impossible to go back to sleep
again, her mind fresh and alert and raring to go.

She pulled her thick towelling robe on over her nightie
and padded along to the bathroom. Keir and Janice's
open doors bore evidence to the fact she was alone in
the flat. It couldn't be much fun to have to turn out in
the middle of the night, she thought reflectively, although no doubt the soft summer nights were far better
than the stark chill of winter on tired bones. Keir worked
too hard, though; it had been evident in the lines of
tiredness etched round his mouth as they had talked last
night—

She caught her thoughts abruptly. It was no business
of hers how long or hard he worked, she told herself
grimly. None at all. He had offered her a room because
it was vacant for the moment and she had been in need.
He had his own life which seemed to suit him just fine;
she would be nothing more than a passing shadow in
the overall scheme of things.

62

She ventured into the kitchen, making herself a cup of instant coffee and taking it into the lounge where she curled up in a big, comfortable easy chair close to the window, her eyes on the sleeping village as she sipped the hot, fragrant liquid. A small milk-float was making early morning deliveries among the winding streets far below, and she watched its progress idly, her tiny feet tucked under the folds of the robe and her hands cupped round the warm mug.

Her mother could be down there somewhere, breathing, talking, laughing, *living*, without any knowledge that her own flesh and blood was just within reach. How would she react when the daughter she had hoped to get rid of confronted her? With anger that she had been found out? Embarrassment? Confusion? Shame? Fury? There was a pain like a knife turning in her heart, and she took a big gulp of the burning hot coffee, shutting her eyes tightly for a moment as though to blank her mind.

She wasn't going to cry again, she told herself fiercely. She was past all that; *she was.* If she had learnt anything from the last twenty-one years it was that the old cliché 'Laugh and the world laughs with you; weep, and you weep alone' was painfully true. And yet... Her eyes were drawn to the village again... She had always felt there was someone looking out for her, keeping her, giving her the strength to follow through on her own convictions and desires, and that certainty had never been so strong as in the last few weeks. She *had* to do this, and now was the time.

The sound of a key turning in the lock brought her out of her reverie and quickly to her feet, just as Keir walked slowly into the lounge, his hard face slightly grey with exhaustion and a grim line to his mouth.

'Good morning.' Her voice was a little breathless, and she heard it with a dart of exasperation. 'Hard night?'

He nodded abruptly. 'Distressing more than tiring,' he

said flatly. 'A case that was doomed from the start.' He rubbed at his nose to hide his emotion, and the curiously boyish gesture from this big hard man hit her in a way she didn't like, causing her to be momentarily lost for words. 'I know in my head that I can't win them all,' he continued quietly as he passed her to stand at the window, his back to the room, 'but that doesn't always help.'

'No, I don't suppose it does,' she agreed carefully. 'Can...can I get you some coffee?'

'Coffee?' He turned as he spoke, his face shadowed and dark in contrast to the brilliant light behind him, and his clothes bearing evidence that he had been out to one of the farms; a smudge of something grisly was on one muscled forearm.

'And something to eat?' She hadn't intended to say it—she had made up her mind last night that the less contact she had with Keir Durrell the better after that intimate dinner for two—but somehow the words popped out of her mouth of their own volition. 'While you have a shower,' she added with a wry smile. There was a definite odour of farmyards beginning to permeate the air.

'That would be great.' He tried to hide his surprise but didn't quite succeed, and to her chagrin she found herself blushing as furiously as if she had suggested something obscene rather than fixing breakfast. 'But only if you eat with me,' he said quietly, his voice devoid of expression now.

She scuttled away without giving him an answer, her face flaming, and once in the small kitchen leant against the soothing coolness of the sky-blue tiles for a moment before opening the fridge.

What had made her suggest she fix him breakfast? she asked herself weakly, pulling bacon and mushrooms out of the well-stocked fridge and reaching for the basket of eggs on the breakfast bar. And when she'd smiled at him had he thought it was in a come-hither fashion, or just the smile of a friend? 'Oh...' She groaned at the possibility of the former, slumping against the wall before jerking sharply upright at the sound of his voice just behind her.

'You haven't done anything wrong, you know.'

'What?' She spun round, her colour surging again at the thought that he had read her mind.

'By being relaxed enough to treat this place as your own for a few moments and offer a starving male sustenance,' he said quietly. 'Both Janice and I want you to feel at home while you stay, I told you that; there's no need to stand on ceremony.'

He just thought she was embarrassed at giving the impression she had taken over, she realised faintly. She would have died if he'd guessed she was attracted to him. *Attracted to him?* The sudden knowledge was alarming.

'And I will have that shower; I guess I don't smell too good.' He was already turning as he spoke, and when in the next moment she was alone again she leant against the stove as a little whoosh of air escaped her lips.

Okay, so she was attracted to him, she admitted to herself silently. So what? Most women would be. It didn't *mean* anything. He had more than his fair share of sexual magnetism, and if her body chemistry responded to the age-old appeal it was purely due to a seduction of the senses, and as such could be controlled. Mind over matter. Simple.

The bacon, eggs and mushrooms were ready to be served, the ground coffee was percolating and the fresh orange juice and toast were already on the table some minutes later when his voice arrested her from the doorway. 'That smells delicious.'

She turned, a polite smile already stitched on her face, and then breathed deeply as her gaze took in the hard, lean body encased in black denim jeans and a pale blue shirt tucked into the narrow waistband, his short black hair still damp from the shower and the very masculine stubble on his chin indicating he hadn't taken the time to shave. He still looked tired, she thought weakly, but that only added to his appeal rather than detracted from it.

He was the type of man who would still look good at seventy, and just at the moment she found that fact distinctly irritating—especially as she was still in her robe with her hair tousled and loose and her face flushed from the stove.

'Can I help—?'

'No!' She interrupted him so emphatically it was insulting, and she hastily qualified her vehemence with a quick, 'There's not room to swing a cat in here; you go and sit down and I'll come through in a minute.'

He made no effort to obey, surveying her with narrowed grey eyes for a long moment before he said, 'I make you nervous, don't I? Is it me or all men? What has happened in your life that you view the world with such distrust?'

'I don't.' She stiffened as he walked the few feet separating them and reached out, but it was only to take the spatula out of her unresisting fingers and place it gently on the work surface.

'You're like a nervous little fawn, ready to bolt at the first sign of danger,' he said softly, so close that her fine body hairs prickled at his male warmth. 'I still find it hard to believe you've been in this big, bad world for twenty-one years.'

It wasn't so much what he said as how he said it that caused her to flush in protest, her back straightening and her chin thrusting out as she stared up into his dark face. So he thought she was some pathetic little helpless female, did he? The sort of woman who wouldn't dare to say boo to a goose? 'Well, I have.' Her voice was militant, abrasive. 'And appearances can be deceptive, you know. I'm more than capable of looking after myself; I've been doing it for most of my life.'

'So you're worldly-wise, a nineties woman?'

He was mocking her, and suddenly it made her hopping mad, loosening her tongue and prompting her to speak before she could check herself. 'Exactly.' She eyed him angrily. 'I know as much about life as you do—more, probably.' Being brought up in the tender bosom of my family saw to that, she added silently.

'I see.' He wasn't mocking her any more; the piercing grey eyes had fastened on her flushed face with an intentness that was disturbing. 'And it hurts?'

'Hurts?' Too late she realised that smoky gaze had seen far more than she would have liked. 'I don't know what you mean,' she lied shakily.

'No?' The last of the mushrooms that were still waiting to join the other food on the two oven-warmed plates were beginning to resemble pieces of charcoal, but neither of them noticed. 'I think you do, Catherine. There was a chink in the armour there for just a moment, wasn't there—?'

'Keir, please. I don't know what you're thinking but I can assure you—'

This time it was her voice that was cut off as he lowered his head, and the kiss was no chaste salutation to a maiden aunt like before, it was a hot, sweet fusing of their mouths that took her completely by surprise.

In the moments before she jerked away she was conscious of the smell and feel and taste of him, the broadness of his frame as he towered over her, the complete dominance and power with which he exerted his maleness over her soft femininity. But then she stepped backwards sharply, hitting her hip on the side of the breakfast bar without even being aware of it.

'Don't.' She couldn't believe the sensations that had exploded through every nerve and sinew at the brief embrace. 'I don't want this.'

'Catherine, I'm not going to hurt you—'

'I mean it.' She couldn't take the gentle, even tender side this big, hard, assured individual was displaying. It was dangerous—far more dangerous than any aggressive battering down of her defences, and she suspected he knew it. 'I don't like being pawed about.' It was deliberate…and unforgivable.

'Pawed about?' In any other circumstances the sheer outrage and indignation on the dark, handsome face would have raised a smile—she doubted if any other woman had ever reacted to him in this way—but as she faced his fury there was nothing to laugh about. 'Paw… I kissed you, woman, that's all. What the hell is the matter with that?'

'I didn't ask you to—'

'You normally *ask*?'

Put like that it sounded ridiculous, but she knew he knew what she had meant. Her voice, shaky though it was, was firm as she said, 'Keir, this clearly isn't going to work out; I think it would be better if I looked for somewhere else and moved out today.'

'Because I kissed you?' he asked incredulously.

'Because… Oh, lots of reasons,' she said painfully. 'I'm not here to get involved, to start… I just wanted a peaceful holiday before I moved on, that's all.'

'Don't you mean go back?' he asked swiftly, seizing on her gaffe with devastating perceptiveness.

'I mean… Look, I don't have to explain what I mean to you or anyone else.' She gathered the torn pieces of her dignity about her with formidable determination as she felt herself backed into a metaphorical corner.

'True.' He had folded his arms across the solid wall of his chest as he stood looking down at her, his feet slightly apart and his big body relaxed, almost lazy. The anger had gone, along with the initial outrage at her accusation, but the calm, expressionless façade was more disturbing than any show of temper, hiding as it did the relentless astuteness of a razor-sharp mind. 'I just don't like to see anyone running away from something, that's all.'

'I haven't said I'm running away.' And she wasn't, if he did but know it, she thought with painful wryness. In fact she had run *to* her problem—or where she thought her problem was, she qualified silently.

'You don't have to.' He gestured to the black, charred remains that were smoking ominously. 'Perhaps it would be a good idea to turn the gas off now? I'll carry the plates through, shall I?'

It was a statement, not a question, and as she hastily put the frying-pan under water before following him into the lounge her head was spinning. Had he accepted she was leaving? she asked herself shakily, trying to bring her whirling thoughts under control. She had made it plain...hadn't she?

He was sitting at the table waiting for her, his back to the window and his hair blue-black in the white sunlight. She padded over to her seat, feeling ridiculous in her bathrobe with her feet bare, but as she opened her mouth to speak, he was there before her, his voice deep and dark and suspiciously humble.

'I'm sorry I frightened you, Catherine—'

'You didn't—'

'It was a gesture of comfort, nothing more.' He had continued as though she hadn't spoken, and the sheer force of his will closed her mouth with a little snap. 'Janice would be somewhat upset if you left now. And your departure might be a little difficult to explain to Sandra and any others who know you are staying here,' he said in such a reasonable tone that she found herself nodding in agreement before she checked herself. 'This is an excellent breakfast,' he added mildly. 'I normally make do with toast and coffee.'

'I...' She was being charmed, sweetly railroaded into doing what he wanted, she thought helplessly. But it *might* look bad if she suddenly decided to leave; she hadn't considered that. And perhaps he *had* just meant the kiss as a gesture of comfort? The thought brought hot colour into her cheeks. Maybe it was her awareness of him as a man that was the trouble, leading her to think there was more behind his friendliness than was actually the case.

Whatever, she had made more than a fool of herself, she thought miserably, jumping away from him like a scalded cat and practically accusing him of attempted rape! He must think she was some sort of nutcase.

'Can I pour you some orange?' he asked smoothly.

'Orange?' She stared at him as though he had spoken in a different language, and then nodded quickly, 'Oh, yes, thank you.'

'What are your plans for today?'

She nearly said, Plans? in the same gormless voice as before, but managed to pull herself together and reply fairly coherently. 'I was just going to have a look around, perhaps take a packed lunch and explore a little,' she said hesitantly, keeping her eyes on the orange juice he had just handed over. 'But about what I said earlier—'

'Take a couple of the dogs with you if you go hiking into the hills,' he said easily.

'What?' She was honestly bewildered.

'Yorkshire is probably safer than the big city—I appreciate that—but a couple of the dogs, or all of them if you feel so inclined, is the best protection I know. They often escort Janice, and they know the drill; they wouldn't let anyone touch you.'

'Keir, I can't impose on you and Janice in this way,' she said quickly before she lost her nerve or he interrupted her again. 'Whatever you say, to have someone come and stay with you is an inconvenience.'

'Is it?' His eyes moved slowly over her flushed, earnest face, the wide violet eyes and silky, shimmering mass of silver-blonde hair, the slim but perfect figure hidden under the thick towelling robe. 'Funny, but I don't see it that way, Catherine.' His voice was deep, husky even, with a smoky, soft element to it that made her toes curl into the carpet.

She drew in a quick breath. He was being kind, just kind, she told herself firmly; she mustn't let her imagination run away with her again.

'If you weren't here I'd have had a solitary breakfast of toast and coffee,' he continued quietly, his voice in its normal cool, remote mode again. 'So you've already done your good deed for the day, okay? So relax now, enjoy your exploring, and I'll think of another good deed for you to satisfy that martyr complex tomorrow.'

'I haven't got—' She stopped abruptly at the mocking amusement in his grey eyes. Why did she let him get under her skin? Why couldn't she be composed and self-assured, exchanging light, careless banter and amusing cross-talk? No wonder he had likened her to a hedgehog—an enormous, great porcupine would perhaps have been more apt.

'All right. Thank you.' She finally admitted defeat gracefully. His will was stronger than hers, and this morning had only re-emphasised the conviction of last night that the less she had to do with Keir Durrell the better. She didn't have the background, the experience, *anything*, to meet him on equal ground.

Keir tucked into his breakfast with every appearance of enjoyment, but although Catherine managed to clear her plate it was an act of will, her appetite completely subdued by his presence. She was painfully conscious of every tiny movement he made, every tilt of that dark head, every muscle in those powerful arms, and it *infuriated* her... But she couldn't do a thing about it.

She had had enough thrown at her in the last few months, hadn't she? she argued silently. Her illness, the shocking revelations by the people she had always considered her parents, the consequential decision to leave all she had ever known and take a great step into the unknown, the knowledge that she was preparing to face someone who didn't want her, would probably be horrified at her appearance in their life—ashamed, disgusted even.

She forced down the last mouthful of food as her stomach trembled. A further complication she just didn't need, she told herself tightly. But why, when her head knew that quite distinctly, did her body seem to have a mind all of its own around this man? And why had he been the one to find her? Why couldn't it have been a grey-haired old man with a fat little wife and countless grandchildren?

She immediately felt guilty at her ungratefulness, and stood up at once to do penance. 'I'll get the coffee,' she said quietly, reaching for his empty plate, 'and do the washing up while you try and catch a couple of hours of sleep.'

'No chance of that.' He stood up with her, big and self-assured, and she knew there was no way on this earth she could squeeze into the small kitchen with Keir.

'Well, you can relax for a while at least.' Her smile was nervous, quivery, and again he felt that dart of burning curiosity to know more—but now was not the time. He had dealt with enough frightened and jumpy patients to know when he could push it and when he couldn't.

'If you're sure.' As he sank back into his seat she knew a moment's blinding relief that was out of all proportion to the circumstances, and just nodded quickly before leaving the room for the sanctuary of the kitchen, placing the plates on the breakfast bar then pouring two cups of strong coffee with shaking hands.

From now on she would make sure she was never alone with him, she told herself firmly, inhaling the fragrant aroma in a bid to steady her nerves. Not that she thought he would look twice at her, what with his wife's death and his busy job that was more or less a twenty-four-hour one from what she could make out. No, it wasn't *his* control that was of concern. She bit her lip hard. It was hers, galling though it was to have to admit it.

The more she thought about it, the more she realised it was her own guilt about her feelings towards Keir that was revealing, even making problems. The kiss hadn't been rapacious—she ground her teeth slightly as she picked up the other mug of coffee—it was her sordid mind that was reading more into his actions than was there. The thought that had materialised before breakfast solidified. So...she wouldn't put herself in a position where she could embarrass herself, or him, again.

He didn't look particularly embarrassed when she walked into the lounge; in fact he looked quite pleased with himself as he took the coffee from her with a nod of thanks, his voice lazy as he said, 'Help yourself from the stuff in the fridge for your packed lunch, and we'll eat dinner about seven, okay?'

'Oh, no, don't worry about me; you and Janice eat when you want to and I'll sort myself out,' she said quickly.

'If you say so.' He eyed her somewhat sadly from under black brows, the grey gaze holding mild disappointment. 'I was just hoping you might be around to help cook dinner. I've a devil of a day in front of me and this morning hasn't been too good a start, rising, as I did, at two. But if you're going to be busy...'

She immediately felt horribly selfish.

'Of course, I understand this is your holiday—'

She interrupted the generously understanding voice uncomfortably, a little uneasy at his carefully bland expression but telling herself she was imagining things again. He wasn't manipulating her; how *could* she think such a thing? And it would be outrageously mean to refuse to cook them dinner in the circumstances

wouldn't it? 'I'd be glad to cook dinner; I didn't realise—'

'Brilliant.' The winsome little-boy-lost façade was
gone in a flash, and the air of satisfaction was strong as
he said, 'Seven, then, if that suits you? There's a couple
of steaks in the fridge, and Janice is picking up some
groceries on her way home so there'll be plenty of salad
and so on. She'll sort herself out, incidentally; she
doesn't like a big meal before she starts work.'

'Oh, right.'

'Do you prefer white wine or red?' His voice was
smooth and matter-of-fact, and she had answered before
she thought about it.

'Red, but—'

'Fine. I'd better go and check on a few of the animals
before morning surgery. I'll just have a shave first so I
don't frighten the patients.'

He stroked the stubble on his chin, the movement
bringing her eyes to his face, and the flagrant masculinity
that was all the more devastating for being utterly natural
made her weak. 'Yes, of course. You go ahead; it's your
bathroom.' She was gabbling, she thought desperately,
and she *never* gabbled.

Once he was downstairs in the surgery she fairly flew
about the flat, washing and dressing in record speed and
throwing a couple of apples and a Cornish pasty into her
old cloth bag, along with a light romance from the doz-
ens in the bookcase with Janice's name scrawled in the
flyleaf.

She crept downstairs quietly, her heart thudding although there was no good reason for it to do so, and
didn't dare take a deep breath until she had slipped
stealthily out of the back door and sprinted down the
garden towards the little door in the fence.

The morning was warm and sunny, the heady scents
of summer heavy in the air as she walked briskly through

the village of Towerby and out into the undulating countryside, following the winding river for some time. Its banks were starred with thousands upon thousands of tiny white daisies and gleaming yellow buttercups, busy insects going about their business of taking pollen as she walked, and she stood for a while in one quiet bower on the river bank, watching the fish darting in the shallows, London feeling a million miles away.

This was another world. She glanced at the hills that were beckoning in the distance. And she had all day, and days after that, to explore it.

For the first time in months a dart of happiness pierced the confusion and darkness, and she breathed in the perfumed air in great gulps as she stood with her eyes lifted to the hills and her shoulders thrown slightly back. She was alive, she was young, and just for the moment that was enough.

She ate her meagre lunch in a small gully where a secret little waterfall splashed its busy way over smooth, ancient rocks and boulders, its water crystal-clear and icy cold. She cupped her hands and took thirsty mouthfuls, the sun warm on her face, before climbing still further. Dry-stone walls stretched in a timeless pattern before her, and the sweet smell of thick moorland grass teased her nostrils as she plodded along, the silence of the windswept fells broken only by the distant bleating of sheep far away.

This was where Keir lived and worked, she thought longingly, in this breathtakingly awe-inspiring landscape. A soul could breathe up here, find itself, *belong*. The word mocked her immediately she thought it. Belong? She shook her head as she gazed up into the clear blue sky. She didn't belong here; she didn't belong anywhere. Her own mother hadn't thought she was worth having, so why should anyone else want her?

She felt the darkness begin to descend and thrust it away angrily. She wouldn't think now, not now; she didn't want this one day to be spoilt by demons from the past. Thinking could come tomorrow and the days after that. For today she would just *be*.

It was getting on for late evening by the time she retraced her footsteps into Towerby, and the air was mellow, soft, the heat of the day slowly draining from warm stone walls and the old, uneven pavements.

She had to walk over an ancient pack-horse bridge to enter the village, under which the water gurgled and splashed over sun-washed stones. She stood for a moment in the dusky air, her nostrils teased by the sweet, timeless scent of woodsmoke as she looked towards Keir's house set in a row of old properties that were above the main village.

'I *will* leave here.' She spoke out loud as though denying a previous statement. 'This is just temporary, that's all; none of this matters.'

She turned and looked back the way she had come, at the great expanse of hills now clothed in the misty blue of dusk. 'And I will manage by myself,' she said defiantly. 'I don't need anyone, anyone at all.'

Tomorrow, or perhaps the next day, she would begin to make discreet enquiries about a young woman who had come to these parts twenty-one years ago. Anna Mitchell. Or perhaps her mother had come here under a different name? It didn't matter; if she was here she would find her—and then? Then the skeletons would be out of the cupboard, she thought painfully, her heart suddenly raw and heavy as she began to walk on. And her mother's cosy little life in this tranquil part of England would never be the same again. She would make sure of that at least.

She found the thought brought her no satisfaction at all.

CHAPTER FIVE

THE concerted barking of several dogs interrupted Catherine's reverie, and as she lifted her head she saw Keir at the entrance to the lane that led up to the row of houses, the dogs bounding round his feet.

She hesitated and then waved, unsure of what to do, but it was a moment before the big, dark figure responded, and then it was just a cursory nod of his head as he waited for her to approach.

'Hello.' Her voice was soft, breathless, and she didn't want it to be. 'I...I'm not late, am I?' she asked suddenly as the thought occurred to her. In her panic to get out of the house before she saw him again this morning she had left her neat little wristwatch on the dressing table in her room.

'Yes, you are late, Catherine.' He was angry. Although his voice was cool and controlled he somehow knew he was angry. 'An hour and a half late.'

'Oh, I'm sorry; have you eaten? Shall I—?' She was gabbling again, and stopped herself abruptly. So she was late, she thought defiantly, but it wasn't the end of the world, was it? He was quite capable of getting himself something to eat, after all. 'Have you eaten?' she asked again, this time quietly and slowly.

'No.' He eyed her without blinking.

'I'll see to the dinner when I've changed.'

'Damn the dinner.'

Yes, he was definitely angry, in spite of the almost conversational tone of voice.

'Look, I couldn't help it—'

'Why didn't you take the dogs with you—or a couple,

77

even one?' he asked evenly. 'Was it an act of defiance against me because I rub you up the wrong way, or just plain stupidity?'

'What?' And then she remembered what he had told her, and he recognised the dawning awareness in her eyes.

'You forgot, didn't you?' It was a flat statement, but not without heat. 'You go tramping off without letting a soul know in which direction you're going—no one has seen you all day—and then you are nearly two hours late back. You could have fallen down somewhere, brained yourself, been attacked—anything—and no one would have been any the wiser.' His voice was rising, she noticed bemusedly, dark colour staining his cheek-bones as he struggled to keep his temper in check.

'Don't you read the papers?' he asked grimly. 'Or is there some divine intervention on behalf of you that the rest of us know nothing about?'

'There's no need to be sarcastic.' There was a strange feeling deep inside her, a painful ache that was slowly twisting her guts into knots. He had been worried about her, he'd made enquiries, he'd *cared*. The realisation was one of anguish, frightening. She couldn't handle it, and the fact made her voice sharp. 'I'm not answerable to you or anyone else.'

'You've already said that line once and I don't buy it twice.' This time the deep voice was steel-hard. 'You're not a stupid woman, Catherine, so don't act like one.'

'*I beg your pardon—?*'

'And I don't buy the self-righteous indignation either,' he continued relentlessly. 'Not when we both know I'm right. If you want to take a hike and get away from it all that's your prerogative—you can walk your feet off for all I care—but you take the dogs with you, okay?'

'No, it's not okay.' She didn't know why she was defying him like this, but she couldn't stop. 'It's far from okay.'

'Tough.'

'Now look here—'

'Catherine.' It was just her name, but it stopped her angry voice like the crack of a whip. Not that he shouted; he didn't have to. There was something in the deep tones that was more effective than any show of rage. 'Stop this,' he growled softly. 'You may not care about your safety but others do; leave it at that.'

And then she did the unthinkable. One moment she was facing him angrily, her chin tilted for battle and her stance militant, the next she had horrified him and herself by bursting into tears. And not gentle, feminine tears either, but great, anguished wails that silenced the dogs as though by magic and caused Keir to freeze for one shocked moment before he reached out and pulled her into his body, settling her against the hard wall of his chest as he murmured soothingly into the soft silk of her hair, his chin nestled on her head.

She couldn't hear what he was saying—her gasps and splutterings had filled her nose and ears and mouth—but she was aware of the gentle rumble above her and the warm comfort of his body as he held her close.

Too aware. As her sobs subsided her senses took over, and along with the awful knowledge that she had just made the most terrible fool of herself was a warm, pleasurable, throbbing ache in the core of her that had nothing to do with her distress and everything to do with Keir.

'I...I'm sorry.' The fear that she might give herself away was stronger than her embarrassment when she looked into his face, but as she leant backwards and tried to move out of his arms his hold tightened.

'Why? Because you forgot yourself long enough to show weakness? To let the real Catherine through?' he asked softly. 'Is that so terrible?'

Yes, it was terrible. It was terrible when it started the sort of chain reaction that was happening in her body, she thought desperately. She had never, in all her life, understood how women could supposedly be swept away by the force of their emotions when making love. Or how girls—and plenty of grown women too—could fling themselves at the object of their devotion, be it a pop star or lover or whatever, and beg to be taken. But she was understanding it now, and he hadn't even *kissed* her. What was she, some sort of repressed nymphomaniac? She groaned silently. What on earth would he say if he could read her mind?

The thought stiffened her still more, but again he wouldn't allow her to break free.

'Well? Is it so terrible?' he asked again, his eyes narrowed on her flushed, tear-stained face.

'Yes.' She wriggled a bit, but he appeared not to notice. 'At least crying all over you for no reason is,' she amended quickly as one dark eyebrow quirked.

'I take it that's a polite way of saying you don't intend to tell me what's wrong,' Keir said drily.

'There *is* nothing wrong.' The absurdity of the statement, considering her tear-drenched face and swollen eyes, hit her a second before he shook his dark head slowly.

'Catherine, Catherine...' Her name was like a warm caress, and she shivered before she could help herself. 'You really shouldn't attempt to tell lies, you know,' he cautioned gravely. 'Not with a face like yours.'

'What's wrong with my face?' She tried to sound coolly dignified, but it was difficult with the reality of his maleness all around and his muscled arms holding her fast.

'Let me see.' He was aware he was stringing this conversation out for his own gratification. He had known she would feel good pressed close against him, so he could enjoy the curves of that small but beautifully proportioned female body, the soft round breasts and fragrant sweetness of her skin. He just hadn't realised *how* good, he acknowledged wryly as he felt his loins stir.

'Do you want a detailed list or a few throwaway comments?' he murmured softly.

'Neither.' The dogs had recovered their equilibrium after her outburst, and had now gathered in a noisy and enquiring huddle round their legs, tails wagging frantically and brown eyes inspecting their faces as first one, then another, would jump up to make sure everything was all right. 'Look, the dogs don't like this,' she said nervously. 'They're worried.'

'Silly dogs.' But he let her go, stepping back a pace and smiling that devastating smile she had seen once or twice that had the power to take her breath away, before taking her arm and turning her in the direction of the house. 'Come and eat,' he said evenly. 'You must be starving.'

Easy, easy, Keir, he cautioned himself as they walked slowly up the incline surrounded by gambolling dogs, the ache of his arousal hard and hot. He hadn't been wrong when he had likened her to a nervous little fawn, and it shouldn't be too hard to display the same sort of patience he would use in dealing with a fearful, tense animal. It shouldn't be...but it was. What he wanted to do— He shut the lid on what he wanted to do.

'Go and have a soak while I finish off the meal.' As they entered the flat Keir's voice was brisk, impersonal. 'Take a glass of wine with you if you like.'

'Oh, I must help.' She followed him uncertainly to the kitchen door, noticing with renewed guilt a prepared bowl of salad on the breakfast bar, and the two, as yet uncooked, steaks under the grill. He had been working hard all day—and that day had started at two in the morning—and she hadn't even been home in time to prepare dinner.

It wasn't *home*. The reprimand was sharp and fierce in her mind. And it wasn't up to her to look after him in any way, shape or form either, and she had better remember that. She could be here a matter of days or a

matter of weeks, depending on how quickly her enquiries bore fruit, and when she had gone he would forget her immediately.

'No need.' He poured two large fluted glasses of red
wine from the uncorked bottle at his elbow and handed
one to her, before turning away to the chopping board
where a batch of large-domed mushrooms were waiting
to be sliced. 'Everything's under control; go and freshen
up.'

Everything's under control? she thought ruefully. She
wished.

Once in her room she surveyed her tear-stained face
and bedraggled hair with a feeling of despair. What a
mess; *what a mess!* She shut her eyes briefly, but the
reflection hadn't improved when she opened them. And
this was her first day here too; he must wonder what on
earth he had taken on. She nipped at her lower lip as
hot embarrassment flooded every nerve and sinew, and
then took several gulps of the fruity red wine to ease the
ache in her throat.

Well, from this moment on she would be the model
of decorum—she *would*. No more displays of prickly
nerves or agitation or tears, whatever she was feeling
inside. She had had years of practice at keeping her feelings hidden—twenty-one in fact—and normally she
managed perfectly well.

She was well aware that among her colleagues at work
and few close friends she had always been regarded as
something of a closed book—reserved, cool even. It had
been the only way to get through sometimes when the
hurt had been so sharp, after some family upset or other,
that she had felt the very essence of her was bleeding
slowly, raw and vulnerable.

So why, she asked herself now as she stripped off her
sticky clothes quickly and reached for her bathrobe,
couldn't she maintain that self-protecting restraint
around Keir Durrell?

She opened the door and fairly sped to the sanctuary of the bathroom, feeling horribly exposed at the knowledge of her nakedness under the robe. But once in the warm, perfumed water she found herself relaxing as the soft bubbles eased away the dust of a day spent outdoors.

After a five-minute soak—she really didn't feel she could spend longer in the water with Keir working in the kitchen—she washed her hair under the shower and hurried back to her bedroom, dressing quickly in white leggings and a long jade-green shirt, before rubbing her hair almost dry with the towel. A few silky silver tendrils curled about her face, as they were apt to do when her hair was damp, but she left it lose, applying just a touch of green eyeshadow to her eyelids before padding out into the hall.

'Refill?' Keir gestured at the empty glass in her hand as he turned at her entrance into the kitchen. 'Help yourself; the steaks need browning a little more.'

'Thank you.' She glanced uneasily at the broad back as he reapplied himself to their dinner. The wine was delicious, but potent; two glasses would more than suffice. She needed all her wits about her tonight.

'So, what do you think of Towerby now you've had a chance to look around?' Keir's voice was bland, his body language relaxed, and she tried to make herself answer naturally, the way someone would if they were visiting for a few days on holiday.

'It's very pretty.' He nodded, but didn't answer, and she waited for a moment before she added, 'I didn't see many people, but those that were about seemed friendly.'

Keir was in a better position than most to know who was who in the surrounding district, she thought with a shred of excitement, but he was too astute by half. She would have to tread carefully if she was going to learn anything.

'It's a working community.' He turned briefly as he spoke. 'Pass me those plates, would you?'

She passed the plates and watched as he deftly served the two beautifully cooked steaks, heaped with mushrooms and onions, before gesturing towards the lounge with his head. 'Shall we go through?'

They had almost finished the mouth-watering blackcurrant cheesecake Keir had produced for dessert—'Not home-made, I'm afraid,' he had admitted with a wry twist of his mouth that was undeniably sexy—before she was able to bring the subject of Towerby's population into the conversation again. It was one of Keir's amusing stories about a somewhat eccentric old farmer he had visited that day that gave her the necessary opening. 'He's never been out of Yorkshire in his life,' Keir finished with a wry smile. 'So perhaps his mistrust of new gadgets is understandable.'

She nodded before saying carefully, 'I expect most folk round here are Yorkshire-born and bred?' Her heart began to thump painfully. It seemed almost…deceitful to be questioning him like this about friends and acquaintances he had known all his life—but she had to *know*, she reassured herself firmly. It was what she had come here for, after all.

'On the whole.' She hadn't been careful enough. 'Why do you ask?' he asked expressionlessly.

'No reason.' A blob of blackcurrant sauce landed on her white leggings as she felt herself flush. Lying had never been one of her strong points; even the tiniest fib had always left her red-faced and mumbling. 'It's just…you must have summer visitors, like me, and people buying holiday homes, things like that?'

'Yes, we do.'

He wasn't making this very easy, she thought irritably. 'And I'm sure some of them fall in love with the place, like I have.' She smiled brightly.

'Have you, Catherine?'

'What?' She was concentrating so much on the real thrust of the conversation that she lost the thread.

'Fallen in love?' he returned blandly. 'With Towerby.'

'Yes, yes, I have.' This wasn't going to work; perhaps she would learn more from villagers, shopkeepers, people like that?

'That's good.' His voice had a brooding quality to it now, his eyes very dark as he stared at her across the table before rising abruptly. 'Coffee?'

Well, so much for detective work. 'Thank you.'

It was almost dark outside, the sky a dense charcoal streaked with pewter-grey, and the lighted windows from the village below giving a cosy, chocolate-box feel to the night. She was standing looking down at the slumbering houses when he returned with the coffee tray, her eyes examining each lighted window and trying to reach beyond to the people inside. She was here—her mother was here. Catherine just knew it.

'Come and sit down in a comfortable seat.' He ignored her hasty return to the table and walked over to the other side of the room where the big, comfy three-piece suite sat, placing the tray on a coffee table in front of the sofa. 'Those dining chairs are hard on the rear end after a time.'

'They're fine.' She avoided the seat next to him on the sofa, and sat down on the carpet behind the coffee table on the pretext of pouring the coffee. 'You've done more than enough,' she said, her voice a little too bright. 'I'll pour, shall I? Black or white?'

'Black, as you would expect,' he murmured cryptically.

She passed him his coffee, taking care their hands didn't touch, but nothing could cushion the disturbing aura of powerful masculinity, the magnetic attraction in the cool, closed face and menacingly lean body. He was the sort of man who would have women turning cartwheels in a bid for his attention and not even notice, she thought painfully. What had his wife been like?

As though in answer to the unspoken question her

eyes alighted on a big embossed photo album at the side
of the CD player, which had obviously been there some
time, judging from the thin layer of dust on its cover.

'A photo album; would you mind if I had a look?'
she asked quickly before she lost her nerve.

'What?' It was clear he hadn't noticed it, and still
more clear he wasn't pleased to see it there, judging
from the frown—swiftly hidden—that coloured his grey
eyes stormy dark. 'Not at all.' Politeness won. 'Janice
must have left it out some time; probably she was showing Michael the regulation baby snaps,' he said expressionlessly. 'She insisted on putting an album together
when our parents decided to move—nostalgia at its most
painful,' he added somewhat heartlessly.

He had been a serious baby and a serious little boy.
Catherine glanced through the carefully arranged plastic
sleeves as her heart lurched and thumped. And wickedly
handsome even then. Janice looked just the same, and
their parents seemed a jolly, smiling twosome, often
laughing into the camera along with Janice, while Keir
stared steadfastly into the lens, his face reflective.

And then she turned the page and there she was, as
Catherine had known she would be—Keir's wife,
Marion, on what was obviously their wedding day. She
wasn't dressed in white, but in a chic pale pink suit and
tiny little hat complete with veil that sat on top of her
glossy dark hair like the icing on a cake. Her face was
lovely, wide-eyed and heart-shaped, and her body was
model-thin, her slimness accentuated by her considerable
height which was just a couple of inches shorter than
Keir's.

So he liked his women tall and dark, did he? Catherine
thought painfully. The very antithesis to her, in fact.

'This is your wife?' She had to say something. She
was burningly aware of his sombre gaze on her face as
she looked at the photographs, and the moment had become charged with tension. It must hurt him when he

was reminded of all he had lost like this, she thought wretchedly. She really shouldn't have instigated the situation, but it was too late now.

'Yes, that's Marion,' he said quietly, moving from his seat on the sofa to sit down beside her on the carpet, looking over her shoulder at the album she had placed on the coffee table.

It wasn't a move she would have suggested. There they were, looking at a photograph of his dead wife on what must have been the happiest day of their lives, a day that had promised a long future together which had been snatched away by the cruel hand of fate. And, in spite of the tragedy of it all, all she could think about was how good he smelt, how close he was...

'That photo was taken on our wedding day, of course,' he said softly, reaching out and flicking over the page. His breath was warm on the back of her neck, his torso touching hers briefly as he leant forward, and she felt a tight congestion in the pit of her stomach that was positively painful. 'This is Janice and Michael—he was my best man. You haven't seen him yet, have you?' he continued quietly.

'No.' She was having difficulty in seeing him now; all her senses were tuned into the warm, tough, male body behind hers, and nothing else seemed real. She forced herself to concentrate on the photograph of Keir and his bride, with Janice and Michael at either side of the happy couple. 'He looks very nice,' she managed fairly naturally as her eyes took in the somewhat small, chunky man smiling into the camera.

'He is.' Keir shifted slightly and she tensed, but the hard frame didn't touch hers. 'But what's even better is that he understands Janice through and through, and manages to curb her excess of enthusiasm when appropriate,' he said with dry, brotherly satisfaction. 'Her heart rules her head most of the time.'

'Does it?' She couldn't tear her eyes away from the tall, elegant figure in pale pink.

'But she was a tower of strength for Marion,' he continued softly, almost as though he could see where her gaze was directed.

'So you were only married for a short time...?'

'Twelve months.'

Twelve months? *Twelve months?* However had he coped?

'But we had known each other for some time before that. Marion... Marion decided to leave college and marry me instead of qualifying; she felt being my receptionist was the next best thing to being a vet herself.' She couldn't quite place the note in his voice, and would have given the world at that moment to see his face.

'She must have loved you very much,' Catherine said quietly, keeping all expression out of her voice by a superhuman effort. She had started this particular ball rolling, she thought numbly; it wasn't his fault it hurt so much.

'Yes, she did.' His arm reached over her again and shut the album with a little snap, and for a moment there was absolute stillness in the room. She didn't dare move; she felt almost as though something momentous was about to happen, ridiculous though that was. But when in the next second the telephone rang shrilly in a corner of the room the disappointment was shattering.

'Excuse me.' As he stood up one hard thigh brushed against her shoulder, and the brief contact was electrifying.

The call signified an emergency at one of the farms, and Keir left within minutes after apologising about leaving her with the washing up.

'No problem.' She smiled at him quickly. It wasn't. The problem would have been both of them squeezing into the small kitchen and sharing such a cosy domestic chore.

Once she was alone she cleared the debris off the table, washed and dried the dishes and restored the small kitchen to gleaming order, and, after pouring herself another cup of coffee from the percolator Keir had switched on, she walked through to the lounge again.

The photograph album suddenly seemed to have become an entity in itself, pulsing gently in the corner of the room as her eyes were drawn to it.

It would do no good to open it again, she told herself firmly. No good at all. She didn't want to gaze at his wife again, look into that lovely face and try and decide what it was about this particular woman that had captivated Keir enough to ask her to spend the rest of her life with him, to wonder how he had felt when Marion had been snatched from him.

She had no right to go poking about in his home anyway, and he had made it clear, by that abrupt closing of the album, that he hadn't liked her curiosity. She was here as a temporary guest, and only because circumstances had thrust her on him and he had felt obliged to help her out. It wouldn't be right to take advantage of that.

She opened the album.

It was nearly an hour later before she closed it again and walked through to her room, her heart as heavy as lead and her face sombre.

She wished she hadn't come here. The thought was savage and strong, and she stood for a long time at the window, looking out into the darkness beyond before pulling the curtains and getting ready for bed, only to lie in the warm blackness for what seemed like hours as her mind churned and spun.

It was stupid—*she* was stupid—to think she could find her mother after all this time. She obviously hadn't wanted to be found; there had been no contact in twenty-one years after all. She was the proverbial needle in a haystack. The best thing Catherine could do was pack her bags tomorrow and leave Yorkshire at once, make the new start she had promised herself. There was nothing for her here—nothing—and she didn't want there to be, she added fiercely.

Yes, she would leave tomorrow. She curled into a tight little ball under the covers, willing the hot tears that were stinging the back of her eyeballs not to fall. Her mother didn't want her? Well, she didn't want her either. She didn't want or need anyone; she could survive on her own. The ache in her chest worsened, becoming a physical pain, and her pillow was damp when at last she drifted into a troubled, restless slumber full of nightmarish images and jangled, elusive half-dreams.

It was two weeks later, and Catherine was still in Yorkshire. She had awoken the morning after the dinner with Keir determined to tell him she was leaving, but somehow the day had come and gone and there hadn't been a right moment, and then the following days had settled into a pattern all of their own almost without her being aware of it.

She rose early every morning, only leaving her room when she heard Keir go downstairs to the surgery. And, after a hasty breakfast, she fixed herself a light packed lunch that included a large bottle of water in her knapsack, rounded up the dogs, and left for the hills.

And so it was that the seven of them spent warm, sunny day after day in the pure Yorkshire air, usually without seeing another living soul, exploring wooded valleys, shallow, crystal-clear rivers, rich, scented moorland and the odd beautiful monastic ruin that Catherine stumbled over in her wanderings.

The dogs were wonderful companions, and were soon quite devoted to this new friend who had obviously been sent from doggy heaven as a ministering angel completely in tune with their needs, from roaming the countryside each day to snacks of biscuits and chocolate when the opportunity arose, as it did fairly frequently.

And gradually, imperceptibly, as her clear, soft skin took on the golden, honey-toned hue of long hours spent in the hot sun, her mind and body began to relax, enabling her to sleep deeply at night and wake refreshed and rested each morning.

After that second evening Janice had finished the night shift and was now back on days, so dinner was a threesome—something that Catherine was inordinately thankful for. She normally escaped to her room fairly quickly after the meal, pleading, quite truthfully, exhaustion.

Not that Keir seemed to notice if she was there or not. It had rankled at first—the distant, almost cold way he had of treating her since that night they had looked at the photograph album together—but she had come to terms with it now; she'd had to. She had wanted him to keep out of her way, she'd told herself over and over again in the ensuing days, so she couldn't very well take umbrage when he did just that, could she? He was a busy man, and more so at the moment as he was waiting for his new assistant—a local lad who had been away at veterinary college but now needed a job—to arrive.

No, she really couldn't complain. But it was just that—ridiculous though it sounded when she tried to identify the feeling that gripped her—the flat, the village, even the countryside seemed to *breathe* Keir. She never really felt as though she could get away from him. He was constantly in her thoughts, popping in at any odd moment she didn't guard her mind, and then staying tenaciously there, obstinately resisting all her attempts to cast him aside. It was more than a little disturbing—and distracting—and consequently she hadn't followed through on any further enquiries about her real mission here.

But she had to nerve herself to set the ball rolling.

She knew the success of her quest would be purely down to her determination, and so, one morning, when she had been in Towerby just over two weeks, she found herself opening the door of the village shop with tentative fingers.

'Hello there, lass. Another grand day again, isn't it, eh?' The little old lady behind the ancient counter, who resembled a small round robin as much as anything, smiled at her cheerfully. 'You're the young lass who's staying with the veterinary, aren't you?' She bobbed her head and flattened down her apron like a bird smoothing its feathers.

'Yes, Keir and Janice.' Janice had already told her that her arrival in the small community would have been noted and discussed since day one. 'I'm here on holiday for a week or two.'

'That's right, lass. Well, you enjoy yourself. Nothing like good Yorkshire air for putting roses in your cheeks.'

She was treated to another beaming smile before the little woman continued to slice a joint of fresh home-cured ham, a half-filled box of groceries at her elbow indicating she was completing an order for someone.

Catherine wandered to the back of the shop, glancing idly at the well-stocked shelves. It was like stepping back in time here, she thought wonderingly as she took note of the old-fashioned layout and big wooden counter complete with a large, archaic till. She had grown up in London with supermarkets and high-rise flats at every corner, a hundred different take-aways within reach at any one point—even the odd corner shop that remained in the metropolis was streamlined and run by sharp-eyed businessmen.

But here, with the delicious smell of ham and bread permeating the shop, and a glass cabinet displaying cheeses, cold meats and little pots of home-made pickles, she could hardly believe she was in the twentieth century.

She reached for a bar of chocolate and walked back to the counter, deciding she would stock up the fridge in the flat with some ham and cheese and salad stuff before she went for her walk today. Keir wouldn't let her pay anything for her board and lodging, although she had already decided she would leave a healthy cash thank-you when she left. *When she left.* She thrust the sudden, sick feeling aside and made her requests known to the little shopkeeper.

'It's lovely round here, isn't it?' She wondered how she could bring the conversation round to the real point of her visit. 'The scenery is quite magnificent.'

'Aye, it is that, lass, although it's the same old story,' the small woman said cheerfully. 'Them's that are born and bred here see the other side of things. The winters are hard; we're snowed in for weeks hereabouts in the worst of it.'

'Are you?' Catherine saw her opportunity and took it. 'But you still get people moving here, so I guess it doesn't put everyone off. I seem to remember my parents saying someone they knew moved to this very village some years ago.'

'Oh, aye? When was that, then?' The little shopkeeper put the pound of ham she had sliced into a greaseproof bag and reached for the slab of creamy white cheese Catherine had selected, cutting and weighing a generous portion on the gleaming old scales.

'About...' Catherine licked suddenly dry lips and aimed for nonchalance. 'About twenty, twenty-one years ago, I think; something like that. Her name was Anna.'

'Anna?' There was a quick shake of the bird-like head.

'Well, I've been here all me life, lass, and I don't remember no Anna. The only Anna I know is Mrs Brown's little 'un, and she's five.'

'I think it was Anna; Anna Mitchell,' Catherine said carefully.

'Well, you could be right, lass; there's some that's come and gone who I don't remember too clearly. Perhaps she didn't stay long?' the small woman said brightly. 'Not all of 'em do.'

'No, I don't suppose they do.' Catherine opened her mouth to say more, but in the next second the door was jangling open again and a young woman with two small and very active toddlers entered, shopping list in hand, and the moment was gone.

Once in the street again, her packages in two carrier bags, she stood for a moment or two lost in thought, and then almost jumped out of her skin as a deep voice behind her said, 'You look weighed down, Catherine; can I help?'

'Keir!' Her heart was still thudding painfully seconds later. 'You're supposed to be at Major Gregson's place.'

'I was.' He grimaced ruefully. 'Earning myself a nasty kick between my shoulderblades from a less than grateful patient. That big stallion of his is a bad-tempered brute at the best of times, and me sewing up a gash on his hind quarters didn't appeal for some reason. I went from one end of the damn stable to the other.'

'The horse kicked you?' She was horrified, and it showed. 'But it must have hurt!'

'Somewhat,' he murmured drily. 'The more so because the stablehand is a girl, and the relief of being able to express my dissatisfaction vocally with the animal was therefore denied me. Anyway, I thought I'd better pick up some of my tried and tested standby in this situation—' he indicated the package in his hand that bore the local chemist's name '—before I continued with the rest of the calls. I've learnt by experience you can't apply the stuff too soon.'

'What is it?'

'A special embrocation that's something of a witch-doctor's brew, but works like magic.' He took the carrier bags from her unresisting fingers. 'You're going home with this lot?'

'I'm going back to the flat.' If he noticed the deliberate clarification he didn't comment, merely walking her over to the Land Rover parked at the side of the road and opening the passenger door, taking no notice of her protestation that she could walk.

'You're going home, I'm going home,' he said smoothly once he was inside the vehicle and she still continued to object. 'Okay?'

It wasn't. He was too big, too close and too... everything, she thought weakly, but she could hardly say so. 'Fine.' She nodded brightly, and thought she saw the hard mouth curve slightly, but he said nothing, starting the engine and driving the few hundred yards back to the surgery without further comment.

They entered the house from the long rear garden as normal, but once in the hall Sandra was there as though by magic, big green eyes taking in the carrier bags Keir was holding and Catherine's flushed face. She homed in on him like an anxious mother with a wayward child, Catherine thought with dark amusement, but there was nothing maternal in Sandra's feelings for her handsome boss; she would dare bet her life on that.

'Back so soon?' Sandra's voice was a little too sharp and brittle—a fact the beautiful blonde must have picked up herself, because the tone was blander when she added, 'Anything wrong?'

'No.' Keir didn't pause as he rounded the corner, his hand on Catherine's arm, and began to mount the stairs. 'I've been to Gregson's, incidentally, but the rest will have to wait a while. I'm leaving again in half an hour or so; if anyone calls in the meantime take a message and put it on the list of calls if they can't make a surgery visit. I'll check with you before I go.'

'Right.' Sandra obviously wanted to say more but Keir gave her no chance, opening the front door of the flat as he finished speaking and ushering Catherine through before shutting it firmly behind him.

She saw him wince as he lifted the carrier bags onto the breakfast bar for her to unpack, and the thought that had been bothering her since their conversation—namely how he was going to reach the middle of his back without assistance—intensified. If it had been anyone else—*anyone else*—she would have offered to help, but Keir... Why couldn't the horse have kicked him on the leg? she thought unsympathetically. Or his arm, his chest? Anywhere but the most unreachable part of his anatomy!

Oh, for goodness' sake! The flood of self-disgust was hot. She was sure this small, simple gesture of help wasn't beyond her, especially in view of all he had done for her. She was acting like the worst sort of prude, and it wasn't like her. He probably wouldn't accept the offer if she made it anyway.

He did, with an alacrity that gave her no chance to change her mind.

'It doesn't smell too bad.' He walked through to the lounge, Catherine trailing awkwardly behind him, and placed the bottle on the table before beginning to undo the buttons of his shirt.

Oh, help, he was taking his clothes off! Not his clothes, the other part of her mind answered soothingly, just his shirt. Just his shirt? Her breathing quickened as he shrugged the material off very wide male shoulders, the strong muscles in his neck and arms and his hair-roughened chest causing her to acknowledge that just his shirt was more than enough.

'Right.' Her voice was squeaky in spite of her efforts to sound businesslike and controlled, and she struggled with the cap of the bottle for humiliating seconds before he reached across and took it out of her weak fingers.

'Allow me.' There was a smoky amusement in the deep voice that brought her eyes sharply to his face, but he stared back at her innocently as he handed back the opened bottle, his face suspiciously blank.

'Thank you.' She aimed for dignity, sternly refusing to blush. 'Now where, exactly...?'

'Here.' He turned, the movement causing muscles to ripple across his smooth, tanned back. But it wasn't his body that caused her to catch her breath this time, but the severe bruising—already a nasty deep blue at the centre which was two inches wide—that covered the whole area from shoulderblade to shoulderblade, and was swollen and angry.

'Oh, Keir.' Her voice was faint but so shocked, he turned again, the self-deprecatory smile at her reaction to his injury fading as he saw the real horror in her eyes.

'Hey, it's not as bad as it looks—if it looks as bad as I think it does from your face.' He was aiming for lightness, but for the life of her she couldn't respond.

'You could have been killed—if he'd kicked your head...'

'He didn't.' His voice was very soft.

'You ought to see a doctor—'

'No way.' That was adamant enough.

Quite when in the conversation the bombshell hit her she wasn't sure—even afterwards, when she dissected every word and intonation of their voices—but suddenly she knew, without a doubt, the reason she had been avoiding Keir from almost the first moment they had met. She had sensed that here was a man she could fall in love with...and she was more than halfway there.

'Catherine, I'm all right, really,' he said gently—so gently that she immediately suspected he knew her shameful secret and was embarrassed by it. He must have women throwing themselves at him all the time, she thought wretchedly. Sandra for one, and Janice had hinted there were more who would like to comfort him in his widowed state.

Well, he might take a bit of comfort—most men

would, she admitted honestly—but it wouldn't mean anything to him beyond a brief, pleasurable interlude. She had seen that his work was his life now; he was almost ruthless about his commitment to the practice, and he clearly didn't have time for any emotional involvement even if he wanted it—which he didn't.

'Catherine?' He reached out to touch her but she moved so sharply his mouth tightened, his arm falling back to his side. 'I can get Janice to put the ointment on later if you like,' he said quietly. 'Being a nurse, she's used to far worse than this.'

'No, no, I'm fine.' Control, Catherine, control, she told herself grimly; it's all in the mind. 'I just wasn't expecting it to be so sore, that's all.'

'He's got a powerful body,' Keir said flatly as he turned again.

He's not the only one. Catherine's stomach clenched but she poured a small amount of the pale green creamy liquid onto her hand and took a deep breath as her legs trembled. Oh, he was gorgeous, she thought with a kind of numb painfulness as she tentatively stroked the embrocation over the hard-planed contours of his back, standing on tiptoe to do so. His skin felt warm and silky-smooth under her fingers, his flesh brown and vibrant and alive, with a fresh, lemony smell that was quickly obscured by the faint medical odour of the ointment.

She was unprepared for the rush of sensation that exploded within her, and eternally grateful he couldn't see her face. Her hands moved slowly over the surface of his skin, her touch gentle and rhythmic, especially on the heart of the bruising, and she was shamefully aware of little tremors of pleasure at the feel of his body beneath her fingers.

Unlike some naturally hairy men Keir's back was as smooth as his chest was hairy, his muscled shoulders wide and firm with not an ounce of superfluous flesh to be seen. He leant forward slightly as she worked, his arms outstretched and his hands resting on the edge of the table, his head bent downwards.

She wanted to ask him if she was hurting him but she didn't trust her voice. She had never dreamt in her wildest dreams that the feel of a man's body could be so erotic, so primitively sexy; she was in very real danger of losing control.

And Marion had been *married* to him. The thought was piercingly painful. They had worked together, eaten together, *slept* together, done all the hundred and one intimate little things that made up married life. Had she known how very lucky she was? Catherine thought dumbly, and then felt quite shattered that she could think such a thing about a woman who had died so tragically young.

'Is that enough?' She forced the words through dry lips, but even to herself she sounded feeble.

'Would you mind doing the area on my backbone a little more?'

His voice was strange, husky, but then he was in an uncomfortable position, Catherine thought shakily, dutifully pouring a little more creamy liquid onto one palm. And his back must be aching like mad.

There was something aching, but it wasn't Keir's back. The shy and tormentingly erotic caress of Catherine's nervous massage was responsible for a tide of passion that was causing his blood to surge through his veins like fire, his arousal hot and hard and his breathing ragged. What was the matter with him? he asked himself now. He wasn't a masochist by nature, so why the hell was he prolonging this suffocatingly sweet torture?

'Does...does this sort of thing happen often?' She had to say something to break the lascivious nature of her thoughts.

'What?' His voice was startled, and then she felt him

take a deep breath before he said, 'Oh, the stallion, you
mean? No, not often.'

'I still think you should see a doctor.'

'I don't want to see a doctor, Catherine,' he said quietly as she took a step backwards and began to screw
the top on the bottle. He flexed his powerful shoulders
as he spoke, turning to look at her with narrowed grey
eyes for a moment before he added, 'Thank you; that's
helped.'

'Good.' She would die if he guessed anything—
shrivel up to nothing and disappear, she thought wildly.
But unfortunately, especially in view of the way she felt,
her legs had no strength to move, and her eyes were
hopelessly riveted on the alien hairiness of his naked
chest. She didn't want to act like the naive young schoolgirl he had first accused her of being; she just couldn't
help it.

She knew he was going to kiss her a moment before
he bent his head—well, she had all but begged him to,
hadn't she? she savaged herself painfully. But although
the sensible thing would have been to move away, to
turn her head, *anything* to preserve the last remnants of
her dignity, her mouth was waiting for him and her eyes
already beginning to close as his lips touched hers.

The kiss was hard and sweet, hungry, and as he pulled
her roughly against him she could feel his heart slamming against the solid wall of his chest, his maleness
overwhelming. He moulded her softness against the
primitive thrust of his body, his powerful arms crushing
her into him as though he would envelop her, eat her
up. And along with a shred of panic at the hitherto unknown force of his blatant arousal was a fierce, eager
exultation that he wanted her—badly.

'Catherine, Catherine...' He covered her face in burning little kisses, each one like hot, sweet honey, before
taking her mouth again in a deep, long kiss that made
her want more. She found herself straining into him, her

hands clinging to his naked shoulders and her feet almost off the ground as he held her close.

And then they both heard it—the frantic ringing of the doorbell, followed by loud voices, distraught wails by what was obviously a child, and then Sandra's feet flying up the stairs to the flat.

Catherine had jerked herself free at the first ring, the strident note cutting into her tumultuous emotion, and Keir was already at the door, shirt on but unbuttoned, when Sandra knocked.

'There's been an accident.' As Keir opened the door Sandra blinked rapidly, but continued speaking with a composure Catherine envied. 'A car mounted the pavement in front of Sarah Matthews and little Toby. Toby's okay—he was in the pushchair—but the car took the lead out of Sarah's hands and Bingo went under the front wheels—'

Catherine didn't hear any more as the door banged shut and two pairs of footsteps hurried down to the surgery, where, within a few minutes, the wails stopped and all was deathly quiet.

CHAPTER SIX

IT WAS a full half hour before Catherine could pull herself together sufficiently to venture downstairs, and then she found the front door was locked and Sandra was obviously assisting Keir in the operating theatre. There was no sign of the said Sarah Matthews and little Toby, so she assumed Keir had sent them home to await further news on their pet.

She couldn't have described how she felt to anyone. Part of her was raw inside at the terrifying realisation she had fallen in love with someone who was as far out of her orbit as the man in the moon. Keir was the sort of man who only happened once in a lifetime, and if she recognised the fact it was a sure-fire certainty the rest of the female population did too. Females like Sandra—beautiful, self-assured, with no skeletons in the cupboard and no hang-ups to cripple any emotional relationships.

Add to that the fact that he had been married and recently widowed—a devastating blow for any man—and the last thing he would be looking for was serious involvement after such a tragic, searing time.

He had a career that was much more than that to him—it was a way of life, an integral part of him, a foundation that even the death of his wife hadn't rocked, something rewarding and substantial. So...why had such a man looked at her twice? There was only one answer—she was available, and she had thrown herself at him.

She stood in the hall, shutting her eyes tightly and clenching her fists against the red-hot shame that covered her skin in a warm flush and sat in her stomach like a great, heavy stone.

What must he think of her? She opened her eyes quickly as though the thought were going to conjure him up out of thin air. She didn't really want to know the answer to that one, did she? she thought with scathing self-disgust. He would think what any other man would think in the circumstances—that she was into casual relationships, a good time, whatever. He wasn't to know that he had hit her like a ton of bricks, that she had never felt this way before and couldn't imagine doing so again.

To him the facts alone would speak for themselves. She hadn't even known him three full weeks and yet she had allowed— Well, it wasn't so much what she had allowed, she corrected herself miserably. Nothing had actually happened of any earth-shattering importance, but only because poor Sarah Matthews' little Bingo had been run over. Otherwise... She cupped her hot cheeks in her hands. Otherwise things might well have had a very different conclusion...

She had to get away and think. She rounded up the pleased dogs—who knew the routine by now and stood obediently waiting for the requisite collars and leads to be put on—and left quickly, without even stopping to fix herself a packed lunch. She could buy some chocolate or something, she told herself as she hurried down the garden and let herself and her eager cohorts through the gate, and a packet of biscuits for the dogs. She didn't feel like eating anyway; she felt sick to the heart of her.

However, a day spent in touch with nature and the peaceful solitude of the rolling countryside restored her equanimity sufficiently for her to be able to tell herself that she had blown the incident with Keir out of all proportion as she walked homewards in the quiet of the balmy evening.

Nothing had happened, she told herself firmly as her eyes were drawn up to the row of houses on their incline above the main street of the village, and nothing was going to. This feeling that gripped her—her mind balked at the word 'love' now—would diminish once she left Yorkshire. The last few months since she had found out the truth about her beginnings had been devastatingly painful, confusing, and that was colouring her thoughts and emotions; that was all it was. That was all she would *allow* it to be.

Nevertheless, by the time she let herself into the back of the house her heart was thudding wildly and she felt weak with a mixture of apprehension, excitement and panic.

'Catherine...' Keir was just leaving the recovery room as she stepped into the corridor, and she felt light-headed—dizzy, almost—at the sight of him. 'Are you all right?' he asked softly.

'Fine.' She forced a bright, brittle smile, keeping her voice expressionless as she asked, 'How's Bingo?'

'Bingo?' He stared at her blankly for a moment before saying, 'Oh, Bingo; he'll pull through. Fortunately the car wheels missed his body and just caught one of his back legs, but the break isn't too serious and he's a young dog. It was shock and loss of blood from being dragged that was the initial problem, but that's under control now. Catherine—' He paused and took a deep breath. 'About what happened earlier...'

'I'd prefer to forget it.' It was the tack she had decided to take as she replayed the incident over and over in her mind earlier that day, deciding the only way she could come out of this with any dignity at all was to be cool, calm and composed. The main thing to let him know was that he was off the hook, that she understood without a word being said exactly how things stood.

She had thrown herself at him and he had momentarily responded as any red-blooded male would have done, especially one who had been used to an active sex life that had abruptly stopped eighteen months ago. She couldn't blame him, but she couldn't let him continue to think that a light affair, a brief dalliance, was what she wanted either.

He would expect her to go cheerfully when her holiday was ended, no strings attached on either side, but this…feeling she had for him wouldn't allow that if she got close. So she didn't get close—in fact she took a great big hefty step backwards.

'Forget it?' His eyes narrowed as his mouth hardened. 'What exactly does that mean?'

'Just what I said.' The brightness of the smile intensified until she felt her face would crack, and the light airiness of her tone would have done credit to any acting school. 'It was nothing, after all; we both know that. And I'd hate anything to spoil the friendship I have with you and Janice.' A nice touch, a caustic little voice in her head whispered maliciously. That should settle the matter. 'I'm so grateful for you taking me in when I needed help—'

'Grateful?' His face had whitened, and now his mouth was a grim line in the taut skin. 'You mean you were being grateful?' he asked incredulously. 'You thought I was asking for some sort of payment this morning?'

She opened her mouth to deny the outrageous conclusion her words had led him to, but he gave her no chance to speak, swinging round on his heel and walking ahead of her past the other doors and into the hall at the end of the passageway, the dogs surging round him as he walked.

'Keir, please, listen—'

'I think we've both said enough tonight.' His voice was icy, his face more so, and her sense of desperation increased when Sandra appeared from the reception area like a beautiful genie out of a bottle.

'I thought I heard voices.' That seemed to be her stock line, Catherine thought painfully. 'Mrs Matthews is on the telephone, Keir; could you speak to her?' the other girl asked sweetly.

'Sure.' Keir glanced at Catherine, his eyes stony and cold. 'Feed the dogs, would you? It might appease those feelings of gratitude a bit.'

'Certainly.' She didn't betray, by her voice or expression, how deeply the sarcasm had cut her, acting as though she had taken the words completely at face value and as though everything were fine. 'I'll take them through—'

'I've already got their meals prepared, actually.' Sandra smiled at Keir as she interrupted Catherine. 'I was waiting for Catherine to bring them back, but everything's ready.'

'Good girl.' He didn't look at Catherine again, walking through the door into Reception and banging it shut behind him.

'I see to the feeding of the animals, *got that*?'

Catherine was still staring at the shut door, her senses stunned, and for a moment the import of the softly hissed words didn't register.

'What...?'

'The dogs.' Sandra made no effort to hide the hostility in her voice and face, the sea-green gaze lethal. 'I see to all that side of things. Keir's far too busy as it is, as anyone with eyes to see would know. We don't need someone else coming in and upsetting the routine.'

'Sandra, *he* asked *me* to feed them, not the other way round,' Catherine said bewilderedly, taken aback by the sudden attack. 'And I can assure you the last thing I want to do is upset your routine. I should imagine Keir was trying to save you time.' She could hardly explain the truth. 'You always seem to be rushed off your feet.'

'I don't mind that.' The green gaze didn't mellow an iota. 'It's my job—*my* job,' Sandra added aggressively.

'I know.' Catherine tried very hard to keep cool and calm, but it wasn't easy.

'Just as long as you do. This is a working practice, not a holiday home.'

'Now look, Sandra, it was Keir's idea I stay here for a while, not mine—ask him if you don't believe me,' Catherine said stiffly. She was all for keeping the peace, but enough was enough. 'And considering I'm out for most of the day I hardly think my presence is an intrusion into the smooth running of the practice.' She raised her chin slightly as she spoke, meeting the other girl's hard gaze head-on.

Sandra stared at her for a full thirty seconds without speaking, her green eyes slanted and calculating and her mouth pursed with barely concealed contempt, before she flounced round, calling the dogs into the kitchen in a hard, sharp voice that made their headlong dash for food a little more tentative than normal. As the last one disappeared through the door it was slammed shut with such force that a framed print on the wall in the hall rattled before shuddering back into place.

That was all she needed. Catherine stared at the closed door for a few moments before turning and climbing the stairs to the flat, her stomach churning at the sudden confrontation. If she didn't know better she would think Sandra had some claim on Keir, from the way she acted. There had been something in the other girl's face that went far beyond the actual words voiced. But did she know better? The thought hit her between the eyes, and she fumbled with the key before opening the door with shaking fingers.

'Hi there.' Janice was just entering the kitchen as Catherine stepped into the hall, the fact that she was still in uniform evidence that she hadn't been home long. 'I'm just going to have a coffee—fancy one?'

'Thank you.' If ever she'd needed a dose of caffeine it was now.

As Catherine followed her into the kitchen Janice

turned and smiled sunnily. 'Keir told you the good news yet?' she asked briskly.

'Good news?'

Catherine's voice was wary, but Janice didn't appear to notice as she poured two cups of coffee and handed one to Catherine before continuing, 'About Martin, the new assistant. He can start tomorrow—earlier than expected—which should take some of the workload off Keir, thank goodness. The practice is too big now for one man to cope. Being a local lad, Martin knows everyone too, and having just qualified he'll be all bright-eyed and bushy-tailed!' She grinned at Catherine as she spoke.

'Eager to prove himself, you know? You'll like Martin; he was always something of a comic, and I don't suppose he's changed much—got worse if anything, I expect. Sandra had her eye on him at one point, but then—' Keir's sister stopped abruptly and turned a little pink.

'But then?' Catherine asked quietly, trying to keep the burning curiosity that had flooded her system out of her voice.

'Well, I shouldn't say really—it sounds dead bitchy—but...' Janice paused uncomfortably and then rushed on. 'Oh, I'm not going to be hypocritical, and it's what I think. Sandra was all over Martin until Marion died, and then she dropped him like a hot brick once she thought Keir was in the running again. She's always liked him and made no secret of the fact; I'm sure that's why she wormed her way in here as receptionist. She'd got a brilliantly paid job in Compton, and Keir can't pay her half what she was earning there.

'Anyway, that's what I think,' Janice said again, obviously flustered, 'but I could be wrong, of course.'

Oh, no, she wasn't wrong. Catherine's face was thoughtful as she began to prepare the dinner after encouraging Janice to shower and change. And how did

Keir feel about the beautiful blonde? she asked herself flatly, her heart thudding. But then he'd given her the job, hadn't he? Surely that spoke for itself?

Dinner was a painful affair despite Janice's bubbly presence. Keir was icily polite, his manner one she hadn't seen before and which was overpoweringly intimidating, making it a herculean feat to swallow every mouthful of food. Eventually Keir's grim face and forbidding presence subdued even Janice, and, although Catherine was aware of her searching glance on their faces and the puzzlement she couldn't quite hide, Keir's sister was too well bred to pry.

Everything in Catherine wanted to fling herself on Keir's hard, broad chest and hold him while she explained the truth—that he had misunderstood her words earlier, that her feeling for him was tying her up in knots, and emphasising that she couldn't bear to be a ship that passed in the night, that she wasn't someone who went in for brief, physical affairs. But perhaps it was better this way, with this wall between them. In a strange sort of way it was protecting her against herself.

All day she had tried to convince herself that what she felt for Keir was mere infatuation. She was particularly vulnerable at the moment, she had told herself time and time again as she'd tramped the fells. Her physical illness followed so sharply by the searing revelations about her birth had made her raw and bruised, open to all sorts of strange notions and ideas. It was natural she would search for love—her emotions were sensitised, susceptible; she desperately needed an anchor.

But it wasn't that, she realised now. She forced down the last mouthful with a feeling of relief that the dreadful torture of trying to appear normal could finish, and she could escape to her room. She wished, oh, she *wished* it were that simple, but the bald truth was, the more she had got to know this big, dark, capable man, the more she had discovered things to love about him.

Right from that first meeting he had disturbed her in a way she couldn't explain to herself—or perhaps wouldn't admit, she corrected painfully. If she had found him to be brutal, cruel, cold, would she still feel the same? she asked herself now. But if he had been like that this certain something deep inside wouldn't have responded with such intensity anyway. It was as if her heart had immediately known him, and it was frightening, unnerving, without logical explanation.

First her mother, now this. What was happening to her? Why had it happened? It wasn't fair... Her eyes were burning with tears she didn't dare let fall, her throat and chest tight with a despair that gripped her heart like an iron band. She was all alone, and perhaps this search of hers was self-destructive, but still the fundamental urge to find her roots was paramount. She didn't have the faintest shred of hope that her mother would want to be faced with the product of her teenage mistake, but even that searing knowledge couldn't deflect her from her purpose.

She had to know, had to *see* the person she had come from—hear what she had to say, make some sort of impression on her even if it was painful and caustic for them both. It wasn't a decision born out of logic or commonsense, but a primeval *sine qua non* for her having any basis for a future life.

Oh, she was a mess. She gave a little unconscious shake of her head at herself which a pair of keen stone-grey eyes across the table didn't miss. She couldn't blame Keir, or anyone else, for wanting simple, uncomplicated beauties like Sandra who were all sweetness and light for the man they adored. And Keir had had enough trauma of his own in his recent past to steer clear of involvement and ties—

'If you wouldn't mind...?' She came out of her dismal

thoughts to the embarrassing realisation that Keir had been talking to her and she hadn't heard a word.

'I'm sorry?' Her face was hot as she met the cool grey gaze.

'I asked if you would mind helping with one of the patients,' Keir said calmly, with no inflexion in his voice and his face expressionless. 'Janice has been on her feet all day and she's bushed. But of course if you've something else to do she can—'

'No, no, of course I'll help.' She was just amazed he'd asked her, considering how grim and silent he had been all evening, and it was clear from the look on Janice's face that the brotherly consideration had surprised her. 'I told you before, anything I can do to help. I'm only too pleased—' She stopped abruptly. She was gabbling again and it just wouldn't do.

'To express your gratitude...? Quite.'

Her eyes shot to meet his, but she could read nothing in the hooded gaze beyond a smooth blandness which in itself was suspect.

'Is it Bingo?' Keir opened the front door of the flat and allowed her to precede him down the stairs, and she was vitally aware of the big figure behind her before she reached the silent hall and turned to face him.

'No, it isn't Bingo.' His voice was quiet and deep, the slight huskiness which was intrinsic in it causing a secret little shiver to tremble down her spine.

'It's a little bitch I operated on this afternoon—emergency case of severe pyometritis, a bad infection in her womb. She's not a young dog and her heart isn't all it could be—added to which she had a bad experience as a puppy with her first owners and consequently doesn't like men. Normally it's not a problem, but in a case like this anxiety or distress can labour the heart, and she isn't too good yet. I won't require you to handle her as such, merely to talk to her and soothe her while I do what's necessary. Okay?'

'Fine.' If he'd caught the quiver in her voice she hoped he would assume it was due to apprehension at the forthcoming business with the dog, rather than the effect his nearness was having on her fragile composure.

The little dog was sleepy but undeniably nervous, her brown eyes wary as they fixed on Keir's big frame. But once Catherine began a reassuring dialogue, stroking the small head and bending close to her while Keir silently checked her over, she seemed to relax.

Keir didn't speak until he had finished his ministrations and fastened the cage again, and then his voice was soft and careful. 'Good; she's doing better than I expected. Her pulse is strong and she's more alert than I'd hoped for. If we can keep the post-operative shock to a minimum I think she'll make it.'

'I'm glad.' Why, oh, why did her body persist in remembering what it had felt like to be held close to that flagrantly male, hard frame? she asked herself desperately. There he was, as cool as a cucumber and as formal and distant as the man in the moon, while she was shaking like a jelly inside. 'Can I do anything else?' she asked stiffly as she forced herself to meet Keir's piercing gaze.

'Is that a serious offer?'

It wasn't what he said, or even how he said it, that caused her to become pink and flustered. But, even though she told herself it was her own reprehensible imagination that conjured up the dark mockery in his eyes, it didn't help. The trouble was, the heady aphrodisiac of power and gentleness combined, along with the clean, elusive scent of his aftershave and total control of that strong body and formidable intellect, had reduced her to jelly.

'Of course, I told you, I'm—' She almost said 'grateful,' and stopped herself just in time. 'More than willing to help,' she finished weakly.

His handsome face was perfectly serious now as he

surveyed her with narrowed grey eyes, his arms crossed against his broad chest and his legs slightly apart. It was a stance that did nothing for her efforts to get her racing heartbeat under control. 'And you don't think dealing with the animals would distress you?' he asked softly. 'Unfortunately they aren't always pleased to be under my tender loving care.'

Under his tender loving care. It took more determination than she had known she possessed to banish the picture that had flashed unbidden onto the screen of her mind and reply fairly normally, 'I don't like to think of anything being in pain or confused and bewildered, but I know it's in their best interests to be here. You don't want to hurt them.'

'But it's sometimes necessary to be cruel to be kind.' It was a flat statement of fact, and she somehow felt he wasn't referring to the animals now. 'One has to get to the bottom of the trouble, however painful,' he said grimly. 'Anything else is weakness in the long run.'

'And you're never weak?' she asked feverishly, looking up at him with great, drowning eyes as he moved closer, unaware she had backed to the wall until she felt its hardness behind her back.

'Not now, not in the things that matter. I've learnt the hard way—' He stopped abruptly as she went to move away, both arms coming up to either side of her shoulders to brace the wall, effectively trapping her within his hold, but without any part of him touching her.

'I've learnt the hard way it doesn't pay,' he continued softly. 'Marion knew there was something badly wrong months before she went to the doctor, but she wouldn't face it. She had the idea that to do so would make whatever it was a concrete certainty. We can do that in whatever area of our life we're struggling in—work, health, our emotions. It's running away, Catherine, plain and simple.'

'But not everything is black and white,' she protested

shakily, vitally aware of his male warmth, the sensual
pull of the powerful muscled body and large hands that
could work with such skill and expertise when needed,
but were now securing her as firmly as a rabbit in a
snare. She moved restlessly, but he didn't release her,
leaning forward slightly so his body was just an inch or
so away from hers, his head bent and so close that she
could see the tiny black hairs of his beard breaking
through the hard-planed line of his jaw.

'Not everything, no,' he agreed softly. 'Was it only
gratitude you felt when I kissed you, Catherine?' he
asked suddenly, noting the start she gave as his words
registered. 'Or something more? Something pleasurable,
satisfying?'

'Don't...'

'Why? Why shouldn't I kiss you when we both want
it so much? It's the most natural thing in the world to
give and receive pleasure; the animals know that without
ever having to be told.' Desire thickened his voice and
sent trickles of fire down her backbone.

'Keir—'

'I like it when you say my name.' His breath was
warm and sweet on her face, and she felt almost faint
as she looked into his eyes and saw her need reflected
in his. This Keir was so different from the cool, controlled man of daylight hours; this was the side of him
Marion must have known night after night as he trans-
ported her into the heavens... The thought hurt, but not
enough to give her the strength to push away.

'And you needn't be frightened of me; I don't want
to hurt you,' he murmured persuasively. 'Just relax into
the moment, Catherine.'

'I can't.' But her voice was husky and trembling, and
quite without conviction.

'You can.' He just stroked her lips at first, his arms
still at either side of her shoulders and his body a breath
away from her softness. His mouth was warm and know-

ing, and she shuddered as the kiss deepened, aware that his arms were holding her now, crushing her against his hardness as he explored, almost leisurely, the hidden depths of her mouth, slowly fuelling and increasing her response to him until she was trembling helplessly in his arms.

His lips moved to her closed eyelids, her cheeks, her throat, one hand holding her firmly against him as it splayed the small of her back, and the other caressing the honey-smooth silkiness of her arm before stroking down the length of her torso, his sensual touch causing her body to tighten and swell with an alien warmth that was all sensation.

'You see?' His voice was deep and throaty. 'You see how it could be?'

Oh, yes, she saw all right, she thought frantically as she caught at some thread of reason to fight the desire that had turned her fluid in his arms.

Perhaps if she had come from a happy, secure background and were here on holiday as Keir thought, if she had no dark secret that could well cause a miniature explosion in this quiet little community, if she hadn't fallen in love with him—which would make it impossible to walk away when the fun was finished—perhaps then she might have gone with the flow and given fate her hand whatever the consequences.

But there were far too many perhapses.

She jerked aside, the movement so sudden and fierce it took him by surprise, and she seized on his momentary disadvantage by taking another step backwards away from him, feeling safer once she was out of arm's reach. 'Please, Keir, I just came down here to help you.'

She tried to speak calmly, as though her heart weren't pounding in her throat so hard she felt it would choke her, but her white face and over-bright eyes spoke their own story to the man watching her so closely.

'You did—help me, that is,' he drawled mockingly,

the lazy amusement in his voice covering white-hot frustration. What was it about him that she found so threatening? he asked himself angrily. Or was it all men? She had been there with him for a minute—he had felt it, tasted it, damn it!

'This is Bingo.' He broke the unbearable tension by turning and indicating one of the cages where a mournful-looking mongrel was lying with one leg stretched out in plaster. 'He'll be going home tomorrow. And this is Mopsy; most of her problems have been caused by an over-indulgent owner who persists in treating her as a human rather than a cat and feeding her all the wrong things...'

He continued to talk about each occupant of the blanket-lined cages, his manner easy and light, and Catherine found herself staring at his profile as anger was added to the pain and turmoil raging in her breast. How dared he, how *dared* he be so nonchalant and unmoved when she was being torn apart inside? Their embrace had clearly meant nothing to him, had been just a brief flirtation, an indulgence of a physical attraction that could obviously be turned on and off like a tap as far as he was concerned.

She found she was biting her lip so hard there was the salty taste of blood in her mouth, and she quickly schooled her features into blankness as he turned to face her, her voice flat and even.

'Janice tells me your new assistant is starting tomorrow?' Two could play at this game, she thought painfully. There was no way on earth she was going to betray, by word or gesture, how much she was hurting. 'Martin?'

'And not a day too soon.' He indicated for her to leave the room as he continued, 'Hopefully I might find time to pick up some sort of social life again; I haven't had time to breathe the last few weeks since the other guy left.'

And I bet I can guess who will be first in line to help you relax, she thought tightly as Sandra's beautiful, feline face swam over the screen of her mind.

'All work and no play?' Her voice was too bright; if she could hear it so could he.

'Exactly.' He was just behind her as she climbed the stairs to the flat, and she had never been so conscious of her body, almost stumbling up the last few. 'Perhaps you might like to come out one night for a meal?' he asked casually as they reached the dusky landing and he opened the door. 'We could catch a film first, or go for a drive—see a little local colour?'

'I don't think so.' Her smile was brittle as she faced him. 'I'm normally exhausted from a day exploring; all I want to do when I get back is have a hot bath and go to bed.'

'As you wish.' The ice-man was back in an instant, the distant formality he did so well settling over him like a cloak and masking all expression, the ardent lover of a few minutes before a million miles away. 'I'm sorry to have delayed you tonight; it won't happen again.'

'Oh, I didn't mean...' But he had already passed her after shutting the front door, walking into the lounge without bothering to see if she followed.

She stood irresolutely in the hall for endless seconds, and then walked slowly to her room, shutting the door behind her very quietly and then falling onto the bed in a paroxysm of weeping that was quite silent, but none the less agonising for it.

CHAPTER SEVEN

'SO YOU'RE the mysterious Catherine I've been hearing about. I'm very pleased to meet you.'

Martin's introductory speech caused Catherine to stare at him intently, seeking some veiled meaning behind his words, but the good-looking, blond-crowned face was without guile as he grinned at her, and she realised it was just an opening line, nothing more.

'Hardly mysterious.' She smiled back. 'I'm sure you get hundreds of holidaymakers down here in the summer.'

'Perhaps, but they don't all look like you do.' The sky-blue eyes were frankly appreciative. 'You've caused quite a little stir along the local lads,' he continued, before Keir's cool voice interrupted him, the tone icy.

'If you're ready, Martin?' He indicated the door leading to the reception area and consulting rooms. 'There are some points I'd like to go over before morning surgery.'

'Right.' Martin seemed quite unperturbed by his new boss's high-handedness, but Catherine stiffened, her hackles rising. She had waited in her room this morning, after rising early from a troubled, restless sleep and watching a warm, pink-edged dawn banish the black shadows of night, until she heard Keir leave the flat and go downstairs.

She had thought her departure from the house would go unnoticed, but as luck would have it Keir and Martin had appeared from the recovery room just as she'd reached the bottom of the stairs with a view to rounding up the dogs.

Her first impression of Martin had been something of a surprise; he was good-looking—very good-looking—with thick blond hair and vivid blue eyes, his broad physique and warm, easy manner undeniably attractive. But he had hardly said two words before Keir had intervened, she thought now, almost as though she wasn't worth talking to. It shouldn't rankle but it did—unbearably—and she had just determined to say something more when the front door opened to reveal Sandra standing in the aperture, her right hand and arm swathed in bandages, made all the more noticeable by the sleeveless dark blue dress she was wearing.

'Sandra?' Keir was immediately at her side although Catherine noticed Martin hadn't moved. 'What on earth...?'

'I fell down the stairs at home.' Keir was treated to a brave, winsome smile before Sandra continued, 'Silly, I know, but I caught my foot in a loose stair rod. I'm afraid I've torn some ligaments and so on, so it will be a few days before I can work as normal—'

'You mustn't work at all,' Keir said firmly. 'You should never have come in. Go home and rest; we'll manage here.'

'Oh, no, really, I'd prefer to be here.' Sandra managed another valiant little smile. 'I thought perhaps, if Catherine doesn't mind, she could work with me for a day or two—do some of the typing and the things I'd find difficult. It won't be for very long—' she turned to Catherine now with a gentle little appealing gesture as though Catherine had already refused '—but it would mean things could carry on more or less as normal, and this is such a busy time for Keir.'

'Of course I'll help.' Catherine tried desperately to conceal her amazement that Sandra had suggested it in view of what had transpired the day before, not to mention the other girl's seething antagonism from day one. 'I'd love to, really.'

Keir was frowning, his eyes narrowed. 'There's no need. I can call Mrs Napier; she is always available to stand in for Sandra if necessary—'

'She's away on holiday at her sister's.' Sandra's voice sounded almost satisfied, and again Catherine found herself studying the other girl's face. If she didn't know better she would have thought Sandra *wanted* her in the surgery, but that was ridiculous. It was only last night she had been warned off in no uncertain terms. 'And we're terribly busy at the moment, Keir.'

He didn't want her, he clearly didn't want her, Catherine thought with a stab of pain in her heart region. But it was the original catch-22 scenario, and other than being downright rude there was no reason to refuse her help.

'So, two new employees all in one day.' Martin's voice was jolly, with the sort of brightness that was meant to cover an awkward situation. 'Hello, Sandra.' He moved in front of Catherine and nodded at the beautiful blonde. 'You're still working here, then?'

'As you can see.' Sandra smiled, but it was totally without warmth, and it dawned on Catherine that her helping Sandra wasn't the only difficult situation within these four walls. The other girl had thrown Martin over for Keir, and surely Martin was aware of that? She felt a moment's deep sympathy for Keir's assistant, and wondered if he still cared for the beautiful young woman looking at him with such cool composure. She hoped not; he seemed too nice for the shallow blonde.

The next few days were strange, surreal, although Catherine couldn't put her finger on what was troubling her so much. Martin was now a regular fixture in the practice, and was already taking a load off Keir's shoulders. He was cheerful, understanding with both the patients and their owners, and had a wicked sense of humour that lightened Catherine's day more than once.

He treated Sandra with a friendly impartiality that showed no signs at all of a romantic attachment, and which made the working day easy, even pleasant.

Sandra, on her side, seemed all sweetness and light to both men and, more surprisingly, to Catherine. She was seemingly grateful for Catherine's assistance, and displayed none of the covert hostility that had been characteristic before her accident.

And yet... There was something. Catherine's brow wrinkled as she walked down the stairs to the surgery on her fourth morning. It wasn't the fact that Keir had clearly washed his hands of her, much as she had to admit it hurt. No, it was tied up with Sandra somehow, something...menacing, threatening even—like a disaster just waiting to happen.

Oh... She shrugged irritably as she reached the hall. What did it matter? What did any of it matter? she asked herself bitterly. All her careful enquiries as to the whereabouts of a young woman once called Mitchell had proved fruitless, and Keir could hardly bear to look at her and obviously wanted her gone at the first opportunity—what could Sandra do to make things worse?

She was to find out in the next ten minutes.

'Feeding time? I'm starving myself.' Catherine was busy preparing bowls of special food for the patients in the recovery room from a list pinned in front of her when Martin joined her in the surgery kitchen, sniffing appreciatively at the five bowls of pungent-smelling food. 'Got any of that stuff to spare?'

'Don't be revolting.' She laughed and pushed at him with the flat of her hand as she wondered, for the umpteenth time, how she could feel so easy and relaxed with him, whereas Keir created a whole host of different emotions, along with an ache of tense, churning excitement that never seemed to fade. If this agony was love she never wanted to feel it again, she thought painfully.

'Revolting?' He stretched his face in simulated disapproval. 'How can appreciation of good food be considered revolting, I'd like to know? It's easy to see you've never been a struggling veterinary student eking out your last two pennies,' he added with a sorrowful shake of his blond head.

'Neither have you.' He had already told her his parents had more than amply supported their only child through university and veterinary college.

'True. Perhaps I am revolting, then,' he said laughingly. 'Why don't you come out with me one night and find out? I bet—'

What he would have betted she never knew, because in the next instant a cold, hard voice from the doorway interrupted them with all the softness of a razor-sharp blade.

'Martin, Catherine, could you come through to my office, please?' Keir asked grimly, his eyes sweeping over Catherine's flushed face for one heart-stopping moment before he turned and led the way through Reception and to the consulting rooms, beyond which the tiny cubby-hole that housed the large old-fashioned safe and Keir's desk stood. She had never heard Keir refer to the tiny room as an office, but then she had never seen such chilling coldness on his face either, she thought nervously as her heart thundered in her chest. Something had happened—something...awful.

Martin was clearly of the same opinion, his silent grimace and surprised raising of his eyebrows his only comment as they followed Keir into the small room where Sandra was already waiting, her face expressionless but her green eyes bright and sharp.

'Keir? What—?'

Keir cut off Martin's voice with a raised hand, seating himself on the edge of the desk before levelling his gaze on each of their faces. 'Sandra informs me there is a considerable amount of cash missing from the safe,' he said slowly. 'Have either of you borrowed some money and forgotten to put an IOU in the safe?'

'What?' Martin's voice was blank with shock. 'Are you joking?'

'I presume I can take that as a no,' Keir said calmly. 'And the same goes for you, Catherine?' The grey gaze was dark and forbidding, like a stormy winter sky.

'Yes—no—I mean...' Catherine took a deep breath and forced herself to speak rationally. 'I haven't borrowed any money,' she said shakily. 'I wouldn't do that without asking.'

'No, I didn't think you would.' It was said quietly, and Catherine felt, rather than saw, Sandra stiffen at her side.

'Keir—'

'And you have no idea where the money is?' Keir interrupted Sandra's indignant voice smoothly, his tone still measured and steady as he looked straight at his receptionist.

'Of course not—at least...' There was a moment's pregnant pause. 'It doesn't take the brain of Britain to work it out, does it?' Sandra continued, with a meaningful glance at Catherine's white face.

'No? Enlighten me,' Keir said with deadly calm.

'Well, it's obvious, isn't it?' Sandra said tightly, her narrowed gaze making her appear even more like a dangerously beautiful cat. 'Martin's worked for you on and off in the holidays and such like for ages while he's been at college, and I've been here for about eighteen months and nothing like this has happened before. So...' She turned and glanced at Catherine again, a gleam of something malevolent showing briefly in the feline gaze before it was quickly veiled.

'So?' Keir asked expressionlessly.

'Well, because of my arm Catherine has been using the safe, of course.' Sandra was rattled at her boss's slowness, and it showed. 'As far as I'm concerned, there's only one conclusion to be drawn,' she said hotly.

'Ah, I see.' Keir's voice was quiet, even soft now as he kept his eyes on Sandra's flushed face, which added to the sense of unreality pervading the room. Catherine's gaze travelled to Martin, helplessly searching for she knew not what, but his blue eyes were wide with shock, and something else—a wariness, a suspicion—as he looked back at her. He believed Sandra, Catherine thought with a touch of horror; he thought she had stolen the money.

'How is your arm, Sandra?'

It seemed ridiculous in the circumstances that Keir was enquiring about her injury, but as he did so Catherine was aware of Sandra's eyes swinging to his face, and it was a moment or two before she replied, 'It's…it's much better, thank you.'

'Would you mind showing me?' Keir asked coolly.

'*What?*'

'I would like you to remove the bandages,' Keir said grimly. 'Surely you have no objection to that?'

'I… Well, yes, I have, actually.' Sandra's other hand had gone instinctively to the bandaged arm. 'I…it's still so bruised, sore—' She stopped abruptly, her chin lifting as she bit out, 'Anyway, what's my arm got to do with anything? We're here to catch a thief, aren't we? There's over two hundred pounds missing as well as some cheques, and I know who's taken it even if you don't.'

'Oh, but I do—'

'Keir, I didn't take the money,' Catherine said desperately. 'I can't prove it, but I didn't take it.' This was a nightmare, a living nightmare, she thought frantically as she looked into the handsome, cold face. What could she do? What could she say?

'I never for one moment thought you had, Catherine.' It took a moment or two for Keir's words to sink in, spoken as they were in a calm, matter-of-fact tone, but then she looked at him—*really* looked at him, without fear and panic clouding her vision—and saw he meant what he said.

'Th—then who…?' she stammered numbly.

'Call the police, Martin.' Keir's voice was like liquid ice. 'I think Sandra will be able to help them with their enquiries; this has gone far enough.'

'*Me?*' Sandra's voice was a screech of outrage, and in that moment she looked anything but beautiful. 'You accuse *me*, when I've worked for you all these months and she's just arrived? Aren't you even going to search her things? Well, I will; I'm not being accused like this—'

'*Sandra!*' Keir's voice was like a pistol shot, and all three of them jumped. 'Not another word unless it's the truth. Make that call, Martin.'

'You're mad.' Sandra had gone as white as a sheet, her green eyes standing out like darkly glowing emeralds in her pale skin. 'If you search her things you'll probably find the money, and that's the main thing. The police don't need to be involved, surely? As long as she leaves—'

'The decision is mine to make and I've made it,' Keir said grimly. 'There's nothing more to be said. A couple of those cheques that have disappeared were handled only by me; I'm sure the police will be able to find some fingerprints to tie them up with the culprit—unless gloves were worn, of course.'

'Gloves?' Sandra's face had a grey tinge to it now, and her voice was croaky. 'I… You can't… *No!*' As Keir signalled for Martin to leave the room Sandra caught hold of the younger man's arm. 'No, stay here,' she said wildly.

'You didn't wear gloves, did you, Sandra?' Keir said with an icy softness that sent chills down Catherine's spine as she watched Sandra's eyes fly to his face. 'Careless, very careless.'

'I...I didn't take the money for me, to keep,' Sandra said desperately, still gripping Martin's arm. 'It wasn't like that.'

'I know what it was like.' Keir's voice was relentless. 'This whole business of your fall was pure fabrication from beginning to end, wasn't it? You resented Catherine being here, you felt your job was threatened, and so you determined to get rid of her.'

'And why shouldn't I?' Any vulnerability fled as Sandra swung round to face Catherine, her eyes blazing. 'I've worked here for eighteen months and everything was fine until you arrived, with your Keir this and Keir that; you make me sick! You might pull the wool over everyone else's eyes, but not me; I know you've got your eye on the main chance—'

'That's enough.' Keir didn't shout, but the tone of his voice was enough to cut Sandra's voice dead. 'So you admit taking the money?'

'I didn't *take* it—not in that way—I always intended for it to be found,' Sandra ground out between clenched teeth. 'It's in Catherine's room, under her mattress.'

'How—?'

Catherine stopped abruptly as Sandra turned to her again, her tone contemptuous as she snarled, 'With the spare key, of course; it was hardly difficult.'

'No, I don't suppose it was,' Keir said softly. 'Not when someone was trusted as you were. Martin, make that call, please.'

'You can't.' For the first time something akin to fear showed in Sandra's face. 'I've told you, I didn't take the money to keep—'

'You did something far worse.' Keir's voice was curt and cold, and quite without mercy. 'You set out to destroy someone else's reputation with a ruthless disregard for the consequences that was criminal.'

'I don't believe this.' Martin sat down very suddenly on a box of tinned dog food which was standing to one side of the door, his amazement at the unfurling tableau plain as he rubbed a shaky hand cross his face. 'How did you know it was Sandra?' he asked Keir bewilderedly.

'Because it couldn't be Catherine,' Keir said simply. 'She isn't capable of anything like that.'

Oh, Keir, don't, *don't* make me love you even more... Catherine felt his words stab her heart, even as they pierced the icy horror of Sandra's malevolence. No one had ever believed in her before and she dared not trust that it was real. The sudden self-knowledge was more shattering than Sandra's vindictive hatred, and she felt its impact right down to her toes. If he had the sort of faith in her his words had implied that might mean what he felt for her was more than a momentary fancy, and it terrified her.

It would mean opening herself up, becoming vulnerable, *trusting* someone, and she couldn't do it. That was what she had been running away from since she had first met him, not Keir himself.

'Keir, don't call the police.' Sandra's voice was small now, and quiet. 'Please, I'll do anything...'

'I don't want the police involved,' Catherine said quickly before Keir could answer. 'There's no need. We know where the money is, and Sandra's admitted what she's done. Can't we just let the matter drop?'

'Is that what you really want?'' His eyes were deep, dark pools as they held hers, and she trembled at his power over her. 'You realise what the possible consequences could have been if we hadn't discovered the truth?'

'Yes.' She drew a deep, steadying breath and forced herself to speak calmly through the thundering in her ears. 'But we did discover it—' you did, *you* did, my darling; oh, I can't bear this '—and it was an act of malice rather than stealing; I don't think it's a police matter.'

'I disagree, but as you were the target I accept it's your ultimate decision.' Catherine felt a fresh riot in her stomach region at the gentleness in his voice, the tone of which altered dramatically as he turned to the sulky-looking blonde.

'You'll be out of here in five minutes flat, understood? And I suggest your next job is in Compton, or even further afield, if you don't want the result of this day's work to become general knowledge. If you come within a hundred yards of Catherine, for whatever reason, I'm going straight to the authorities. I mean it, Sandra,' he added grimly. 'I don't make idle threats.'

'Oh, I'll go all right.' With the threat of the police gone the bumptiousness was back, and Sandra's voice was loaded with venom as she added, 'But you'll see; you'll see what she's like. There's more to her than meets the eye; you see if I'm not right. She might fool you, with her dewy-eyed look and little-girl-lost approach, but you're in for a surprise, Keir Durrell; just you wait and see.'

So saying, she flounced round, yanking open the door using her bandaged arm—with a force that confirmed Keir's theory as to the 'accident' was right—and leaving with her head held high and her eyes blazing.

'That did all just happen, didn't it?' In any other circumstances the look on Martin's face would have been comical. 'I didn't imagine it all?'

'Unfortunately not,' Keir said grimly. 'Are you all right, Catherine?' His voice softened on her name, jerking her to life.

'I...I think so.' She mustn't cry, mustn't give way now; she had to get away and sort out the turmoil in her mind, she thought frantically. Sandra's vindictiveness, Keir's faith in her honesty and the trauma of the last few minutes were all muddled in her mind with the knowledge that Sandra was right—she wasn't all she seemed; in fact she didn't know who or what she was. It had been hate that had driven her to this quiet little village, that and a desire to confront the woman who had given her life, to force her mother to acknowledge her existence whatever havoc it might wreak in her life, and suddenly she didn't like this side of herself.

Keir was different from any other man she had met, and not just in his physical appearance, impressive though it was. He was strong, straight as a die—what would he think of her if he knew the truth, that she was living a lie? She almost shut her eyes as hot misery swamped her.

But her own mother had wanted to be rid of her— she'd counted as nothing to the person who was supposed to love her the most—and rightly or wrongly she couldn't rest until she found her. But Keir wouldn't understand—no one could understand—how this thing was eating her up inside. She was no good to anyone like this; perhaps she never would be.

'Catherine, look at me, please.' She had been vaguely aware of Martin leaving the room moments before, and now the note in Keir's deep, slightly husky voice made her tremble as she raised her eyes to his. 'This whole episode has been a shock to the system—it is all right to show emotion, you know.'

But it wasn't, it was far, *far* too dangerous, she thought numbly. In fact nothing about her being here in Yorkshire was right—not the situation that had arisen with Sandra and the money, nor her secretly seeking her mother with this burning resentment colouring every minute of every day, and especially not her feelings for this cool, handsome man in front of her; none of it was right. It couldn't be more *wrong*. Things had somehow run away with her, become complicated and horribly tangled, and now on top of everything else she had lost Keir his receptionist at one of his busiest times of the year.

The thought opened her mouth. 'What are you going

to do, now Sandra's gone?' she asked shakily. 'How will you manage—?'

'*Damn Sandra!*' The explosion was sudden and fierce. 'And damn the practice too. I'm not talking about that, woman, I'm trying to find out how you *feel*; is that so wrong?'

'No—'

'Then *talk* to me, Catherine. Shout, Scream, cry, if you want to, but for crying out loud break out of that damn ivory tower you inhabit most of the time,' he said angrily. 'I want—'

As he took a step towards her she instinctively stepped backwards, terrified of what she might reveal if he touched her, and he froze immediately, his dark eyes raking her white face as he visibly fought for control. 'What is it about me that you find so hard to take?' he asked bitterly. 'I mean, I'd really like to know. I thought at first it might be all men, but I've seen you with Martin—seen you laugh, joke, even flirt a little—'

'I've never flirted with Martin,' she protested vehemently.

'No? Then what was that little scene I interrupted earlier?' he ground out tightly. 'Are you trying to tell me you weren't making a date with him?'

'It wasn't like that.' He was obviously furiously angry, and she couldn't think why, unless he was more put out by Sandra's sudden departure than he'd admitted. 'He was just messing around, being funny.'

'Was he?' There was a thunderous pause. 'And you like your men in clown costumes, is that it?' he asked with grim sarcasm.

'Now you're just twisting my words,' she said stiffly.

'How can I, when you never *say* anything?'

'Keir—'

'No, that's enough.' A moment after he pulled her into his arms, his mouth came down on hers with a violence that spoke of intense frustration. But almost in the same

breath the assault mellowed, his lips warm and persua-
sive as they stroked hers apart, his tongue exploring the
inner sweetness with a terrible knowledge of what it was
doing to her.

His thighs were hard against hers, his arms forcing
her against his male frame so that her softness seemed
to merge with his masculinity, and she could feel his
heart slamming against his ribcage, the solid wall of his
chest pounding with the beat.

She drank in the smell and feel and taste of him, her
body ripening and becoming moist as sensation upon
sensation shivered ripples of pleasure into every nerve
and crevice, her blood singing through her veins as he
systematically set out to break down her resistance. If
she had been capable of rational thought she would have
drawn back, made an effort to still the fire that was burning so fiercely, but her arms were wrapped around his
neck, her body straining against his as his hands moved
feverishly over her slim frame.

The madness had to end—it was early morning on a
busy working day—but as they heard Martin's voice
calling from beyond the tiny room Keir seemed loath to
let her go, pulling her even harder against him for one
brief moment before raising his head and looking down
into her soulful eyes.

'You see? You see how it would be?' he growled
triumphantly. 'Now tell me you don't want me like I
want you.'

But wanting wasn't enough. Even if everything else
was all right—and it wasn't—physical need alone wasn't
enough, she thought helplessly. Her mother had discovered that the hard way. Whatever Keir might say, in the
final analysis there was no substitute for love.

'Keir, please.' She drew herself up and away from
him, but he wouldn't let go of her completely, keeping
her loosely within the circle of his arms. 'I can't—'

'No, don't say anything—not if it isn't what I want

to hear.' He stopped her with a finger on her lips. 'You're coming out with me today on my rounds; I'll show you more of the real Yorkshire.'

'I can't.' His finger left her lips and trailed caressingly down her throat, brushing her breast and one taut nipple on its journey, making her tremble helplessly. 'Sandra's gone—'

'Mrs Napier is back from her holiday; she's used to standing in when it's necessary. She likes the extra money, and Martin is here to hold the fort. You need a day in the fresh air after this morning's trauma; it'll do you good to meet some of the farmers and their wives.'

'No... No, I—I can't,' she stammered weakly. 'You must see—'

'I promise to behave myself.' He let go of her now, and for a moment she felt quite bereft. 'I can't say fairer than that,' he added with a wry huskiness that caught at her nerve-endings, his eyes dark with self-mockery as he looked down at her.

'You do?' She hadn't seen him in this darkly sexy, teasing mode before; it was as different from the powerfully contained, cold ice-man who had confronted Sandra as chalk from cheese—and dangerously attractive.

'Hand on heart and hope to die,' he said softly. 'Will that do?'

She was playing with fire here—she knew it—so why was she nodding her agreement? she asked herself silently.

'Good.' He smiled, his eyes a brilliant grey in the tanned darkness of his face, and she caught her breath at the sheer, sensual pull he exerted as naturally as breathing. 'I'll contact Mrs Napier, and once she's here you pop upstairs and fix a picnic lunch, okay? We'll leave after morning surgery. And perhaps you'll retrieve the treasure in your bedroom and return it to the safe?'

He twitched an ironic eyebrow. 'Unless you'd like me to come and help you search, that is.'

'I don't think that will be necessary,' she said primly, ignoring his muttered 'Spoilsport' as she left the room.

'You okay?' Martin eyed her anxiously as she walked into the reception area a few moments later, Keir staying in his office to lock up the safe. 'I still can't believe Sandra did that.'

But you believed I'd done it at once, she thought. It struck her anew that but for Keir's discernment the morning's happenings could have had a very different outcome. But she hadn't time to dwell on it; morning surgery was due to start in ten minutes, and until Mrs Napier arrived she was going to have to stand in the breach.

It was just over half an hour later when a small, stout, middle-aged woman bustled into the waiting room and over to the reception desk where Catherine was working. 'You must be Catherine. I'm Mary Napier; how do you do?'

'Oh, hello; please come round. Keir phoned you, then?' The morning surgery had been so busy, she hadn't seen Keir since the episode in his office, and now she wished she'd checked to find out what he had told the little Yorkshire woman.

'That he did, lass.' The bright blue eyes examined her carefully. 'Bit of a do, eh? Don't worry, Keir knows I can keep me mouth shut. And I've always thought Sandra was no better than she should be—too many airs and graces with that one—and it wasn't the job that brought her here in the first place, if you get my meaning?' Her voice was low and conspiratorial. 'Still, there's an end to it now, and I can't say I'm sorry. I've never liked working with madam, as Keir well knows, but least said soonest mended. You plan on staying in these parts long, then?'

It was clear plain speech was the order of the day,

and as Catherine mumbled her way through an explanation that she was here on holiday for a few weeks, she was aware of the blue eyes searching her face.

'You remind me of someone, lass, but I can't think who. You got any relatives in these parts?'

Catherine's heart stopped, and then raced on at a tremendous rate, and it was a moment or two before she could manage to say, 'I think a member of the family—a woman—moved here twenty years or so ago. Her name was Mitchell—Anna Mitchell.'

'Mitchell?' Mary shook her head slowly. 'No, that don't ring no bells, lass, but it'll come to me in time.'

'When it does, let me know.' Catherine strove with all her might to sound casual. 'If it is the same woman it might be nice to meet her before I leave.'

'You definitely planning to leave, then? Keir tells me you're going out with him today round the farms.' It was said as if one thing cancelled out the other, but mercifully the conversation was brought to an abrupt end as a sudden influx of owners and animals arrived and claimed Mary's attention.

Catherine escaped gratefully upstairs and set about preparing the picnic basket, finding cold chicken, hard-boiled eggs, home-grown tomatoes and creamy white cheese in the fridge. She made some ham sandwiches and added two crisp green apples to the feast, along with a bottle of lemonade and the requisite plates, glasses and napkins. And all the time, in spite of telling herself Keir's inviting her along meant nothing, absolutely nothing, her heart was singing.

She could take this one day, couldn't she? She glanced at her reflection as she changed quickly into figure-hugging jeans and a sleeveless white top, brushing her hair until it shone in gleaming waves and fixing it in a silky ponytail on the top of her head, with a few curling tendrils softening the style. She had made it plain she wasn't in the running for a light holiday fling or

brief affair, after all; if he wanted to give her a change
of scene after the dreadful start to the day it was nice of
him, very nice, she told the warning little voice in her
mind.

And now she had the lead from Mary Napier as to her
mother's whereabouts, after all the weeks of nothing.
And it *was* a lead, she was sure of it. She nodded to the
wide-eyed girl in the mirror as her stomach turned over.
Something was happening, things were being worked
out; she could feel it in her bones...

'Catherine?'

Keir's voice broke into her thoughts and she sprang
up quickly from her seat at the dressing table, before
forcing herself to walk slowly from the room, rather than
gallop to his side as she felt like doing.

He was waiting in the hall, picnic basket in hand, his
dark blue jeans and denim shirt making him appear even
larger in the light-coloured setting, and causing her
breath to catch in her throat as the enormity of her love
for him overwhelmed her again with a feeling of sheer
panic.

Fire. She had been right; she was playing with fire.
And if she wasn't very careful she was going to get
fatally burnt, she thought nervously, walking to join him
on legs that were suddenly leaden, the smile that had
been on her face wiped away as though by magic.

CHAPTER EIGHT

'DOES the soul good, doesn't it?' Keir's voice was deep and soft and he didn't open his eyes as he spoke, his long, lean body stretched out on the big checked car rug and his hands resting behind his head, emphasising his broad, muscled chest in a way that Catherine was finding hard to ignore.

The remains of the picnic had been devoured in seconds flat earlier by the dogs, who were now cavorting in play in a deep grassy hollow beneath the idyll on top of a hill, where a vista of gently roving fells broken by a glinting river winding tantalisingly among great, spreading tees and ancient stone walls could be seen in the distance below them.

Yes, it did the soul good. Catherine glanced at the dark man lying by her side and wondered why, in the midst of such beauty and with Keir so close, she wanted to cry and cry and cry. Perhaps because catching a glimpse of heaven and knowing it wasn't for her was too much to take. She wanted him. She wanted him so much she ached with it, but she was too much of a coward to follow her heart and let the consequences take care of themselves. If he rejected her too—a week, a month, a year from now—she wouldn't be able to stand it. And why wouldn't he? Everyone else in her life so far had. Why should Keir be any different?

She hugged her knees tighter to her chest as her eyes returned to the dogs, engaged in a crazy game of tag, but she knew the second that Keir opened his eyes and lay watching her.

'You're so beautiful, you know. You do know, don't

136

you?' he asked softly. 'With your sapphire-blue eyes and hair like spun silver, I can't think of anything else but you. You're getting in the way of even the most mundane things I do. I think I'm concentrating and then you're there in front of me, with your tiny, perfect shape and shy smile. There's times I think I'm going mad.'

'Keir, don't—'

'I can't help it. I'm not even sure if you like me.' He rolled over and raised himself on his elbows, his chin propped on his hands as the devastating grey gaze raked her face. 'Oh, I know you are attracted to me—physically, that is—but you've fought that every inch of the way, haven't you? Why? What are you so frightened of?' he asked huskily. 'I'm not a monster, Catherine.'

'I'm not frightened.' It was a lie, and not even a convincing one. 'And I'm not trying to fight you, Keir.'

'I think you are.' The softness had gone, his voice a low growl. 'Is it because we both know that if I started to make love to you, *really* make love to you, you would turn to fire in my arms and there would be no thought of holding back? You want me, Catherine; your body tells me so every time I so much as touch you.'

It wanted him now, her breasts ripening and her skin growing hot at the naked desire in his voice. It was her weakness that made her voice sharp as she said, 'And you think that's enough? Physical attraction, lust, call it what you will? Even certain segments of the animal kingdom operate better than that.'

'No, I don't think that is enough, but we're talking about you, not me,' he said with soft intent.

She stared at him, willing herself not to fall prey to the dark sensuality reaching out to her. How did she manage this, him, *herself*? He had been married, and no doubt he had had other women before his wife. He had a sexual knowledge she knew nothing about. She had no skill, no sophistication; she knew nothing about the little tricks women like Sandra would use to keep a man interested once the initial craving had been satisfied. All she had was herself, and it wouldn't be enough to hold him; she knew it wouldn't. It was the only thing she *was* sure about.

He had said he wanted her, that she was driving him mad, that he thought she was beautiful—but not once had the word 'love' been mentioned, not even as a gesture of convention when he was making love to her.

'You said...you said you wouldn't—'

'Make love to you?' he interrupted roughly. 'But I'm not, am I? I'm talking to you, that's all. But of course if you've changed your mind...'

'I haven't.' She frowned at him, her eyes wary.

'Pity.' His smile was sardonic, brooding, and the tilt of his mouth brought a tingle to her own lips, almost as though he had kissed her. 'I'm learning that with you it's better to act first and ask questions later; you need to be taken by storm.'

'I don't need to be taken any way.' She tried to sound severe, but like several times before his mood had undergone a lightning change, and the wry amusement evident in the handsome face was hard to resist. Manipulation? It could well be...

'We'll have to differ on that point, but for the moment this...interesting interlude will have to take second place to Frank Marley's young heifers.' The transformation was complete. He had gone from ardent admirer to angry lover, followed by a dose of dark, self-mocking amusement, and now it was the authoritative, cool figure of working hours that faced her, his dark gaze unreadable as it held hers and the hard angles of his face attractive but remote.

How could he turn on and off like that? she asked herself with more than a touch of testiness. Was it due to an impressive single-mindedness? Or was his pursuit of her merely an amusing and interesting diversion for a short while? She didn't know. She didn't have a clue what made him tick, and—

'Come on.' She realised too late he had stood up and was offering her his hand, his grey eyes narrowed against the white sunlight sweeping the fells and his hair blue-black in the brilliant light. 'And stop frowning; it won't do my reputation any good if you spend the afternoon with a face like a wet weekend.'

'And you have one? A reputation, that is?' she asked tartly, letting go of his hand as though it had burnt her once she was on her feet and pretending to brush imaginary grass from her jeans.

She hadn't expected a serious answer to what was only a somewhat astringent retort on her part, but he straightened from picking up the car rug, purposely blocking her route to the Land Rover as he said, 'I did have, once; you're bound to hear about my wild youth sooner or later so it might as well be sooner.' His voice was cool and mocking, and she wasn't really sure if he was teasing at first.

She eyed him warily, her face expressing her uncertainty, and he acknowledged her unease with a wry shrug of his wide shoulders. 'Of course, it wasn't as bad as people liked to make out,' he said smoothly, one dark eyebrow quirking mockingly as it dared her to disagree.

'Oh, of course.' Her voice was waspish, but she couldn't help it—the thought of him with other women had the little green-eyed monster dancing crazily in her chest.

'Yorkshire is the same as anywhere else. People always love to put two and two together and make ten,' he continued evenly as though she hadn't spoken. 'I had a wide circle of friends at university, male and female, and inevitably different ones would visit from time to time and come home with me for breaks and a taste of home cooking.'

'Male and *female*,' she repeated with scathing sweetness.

'Just so.' The grey eyes were laughing at her, and she could have hit him. 'The gossips had a field day; it was a bit of interest for them after all, and something aside from the normal daily routine. But if I'd slept with all the girls accredited to me I'd be worn out by now... And I'm not.' The pregnant pause accompanied by the smoky amusement in the dark gaze had her stomach muscles clenching.

'Really?' The word carried a dignified coolness. 'I don't know why you are telling me all this, Keir.'

'I think you do.' The amusement had gone. 'That little brain of yours has enough weighed against me without more being added to it. I don't like promiscuity in either gender—I never have; neither have I slept around. Do you believe that?'

'It's nothing to do with me—'

'Do you believe it, Catherine?' he asked persistently. 'A simple yes or no will suffice.'

He wasn't going to let it drop, and as she stared back at him, her eyes wide and steady, she knew it would be fatal to let him see how much this conversation was hurting her. She didn't want to think of him with other girls, women—and that included Marion. It was unreasonable to feel jealous—ridiculous, in fact—but she couldn't help it.

'So you're whiter than white?' She hid behind a light smile and a casual shrug.

'I didn't say that,' he said calmly. 'I've never pretended to be an angel, just an ordinary man with my own moral code and my own set of ethics which I endeavour to live by. There are some things in my past I'm not proud of, but hopefully they've made me wiser.'

'I see.' She didn't have the nerve to ask what they were.

'You don't sound too sure.' He stared at her a moment

longer, and then turned and walked over to the Land
Rover, opening her door and helping her inside before
saying, his voice lazy, 'But don't worry; I don't turn
into a werewolf at the stroke of midnight.'

The dogs came immediately Keir called them, like the
well-trained animals they were, and once they were on
their way again Catherine pretended to look out of the
window as her mind buzzed with all that had been said.
He was being honest with her—very honest. What would
he say if he knew the reason for her being here was one
great big lie? Should she tell him? Her stomach churned
at the prospect, and she shut her eyes tightly before
opening them to gaze at the blue expanse of sky above.
She couldn't; she just couldn't.

He would be surprised and disappointed she had kept
up the deceit for so long, and worse still, he might just
pity her too. That really would be the last straw. As
things were now, if he remembered her at all when she
had gone it would be as someone he'd liked, wanted,
been attracted to, and that image was one she desperately
wanted to keep intact. To have it tainted with pity...she
wouldn't be able to bear it. If she couldn't have him, to
be remembered as the one who had got away, forever
desirable, was all the comfort she would have through
the long, lonely years without him.

Was that awful, wicked? She breathed deeply to control her racing heartbeat. She didn't know—perhaps it
was—but it was the way she felt. She was a mess inside,
muddled, hurting, but he didn't know that, and that was
the way she wanted it to remain. It might be foolish and
proud, but it was all she had.

She glanced at him now out of the corner of her eye,
unaware that he had noticed her peeping until he said,
his voice very dry and sardonic, 'Catherine, I'm sure it's
unintentional, but you're making me feel like the worst
lecher this side of the channel—which is severely testing
the old adage about honesty being the best policy. The

farm's up ahead; could you do us both a favour and relax?'

Frank Marley's farm was small and compact, and Catherine stayed in the Land Rover while Keir went into one of the big barns to inspect the ailing heifers. The grimy farmyard had clearly had animals housed on the big flagstones prior to their arriving, and there wasn't a clear path to tread through the muck and grime, the prevailing odour overpowering.

By comparison, the next farm they visited was a grand affair, with pristine buildings, neat, smart pens outside, and a general air of prosperity that sat well on the big cheerful owner and his attractive grey-haired wife.

'These are my godparents, Martha and Bill Alton,' Keir said in a low undertone as he drew up outside the impressive-looking stone farmhouse, where the middle-aged couple were deep in discussion with a couple of burly farmhands. 'They'll expect to be introduced to you.'

'Will they?' But she had no time to ask more before Martha and Bill were at their side. Introductions were brief; there were a large number of sheep penned and waiting to be inoculated. Whilst Keir, Bill and the two farmhands dealt with the animals Martha insisted on making Catherine a coffee in the gleaming, surprisingly high-tech farmhouse kitchen.

'I understand you're stayin' with Keir and Janice, lass?' Martha said over her shoulder as she bustled about, preparing a tray for the men. 'Grand young man, is Keir, and a brilliant vet. My Bill wouldn't have anyone else to see to his stock. You known him long, then?' It was the sort of direct approach Catherine was getting used to in Yorkshire, where everyone said exactly what they meant and flowery speeches were unheard of, but as she explained the circumstances that had led her to Keir's home she found herself becoming acutely uncomfortable under the older woman's tight scrutiny.

'So you're just here on a visit, then?' Martha deftly cut a giant fruitcake into large slices as she talked, before adding it to the tray along with four mugs of coffee.

'Yes.' Catherine sensed criticism but was powerless to understand why. And although the conversation progressed fairly naturally once the farmer's wife had returned from taking the tray to the men the feeling persisted that Martha wasn't happy to see her with Keir, making her stammer over her words and fumble her replies.

'Bad business with Marion.' It was straight out of the blue; they had been discussing the good works of the Women's Institute, of which Martha was a stalwart member, moments before. 'You know he cared for her himself at home right up to the end?'

'No, I didn't; I don't know too much about it,' Catherine said uncomfortably.

'Marion was petrified of hospitals.' Martha's body language expressed disapproval which was confirmed by her next words. 'Put a tremendous strain on Keir, with him having taken on the practice and all. Between Marion and the surgery he wore himself into the ground. But there you are; he wouldn't have it any other way. He can be very stubborn, you know.' She looked straight into Catherine's eyes now. 'But we think the world of him, me and Bill. I wouldn't like to see him hurt again.'

'No...' It dawned on Catherine that she was being warned off, in no uncertain terms, and for a moment she didn't know whether to be angry, offended or just plain hurt that Martha obviously found her so wanting. She settled on a mixture of all three. 'I'd hate to see him hurt too, Martha.'

There was an inflexion in Catherine's voice, of which she was completely unaware, that had the older woman's eyes sharpening on her face. It was a full thirty seconds before Martha said, her voice soft now and quiet, 'That's good, lass, because I've got an idea—'

What Martha's idea was Catherine never discovered, because in the next moment the kitchen door opened with gusto as Bill and Keir entered, and within minutes she and Keir were seated in the Land Rover again and on their way.

'What's wrong?' Keir's voice was flat, and Catherine realised she had said nothing for the last five minutes, having drifted off into a world of her own as she worried at all Martha had said like a dog with a bone. Having lived with condemnation and discouragement all her life, it took little to make her doubt herself, and now she found she couldn't throw off the weight Martha had placed on her shoulders, try as she might.

'Wrong? Nothing's wrong,' she lied brightly. 'I was just enjoying the beautiful scenery—'

'Did Martha say something to upset you?' He refused to accept the weak prevarication with a firmness that was formidable. 'She can be a little…forthright at times, but her heart is as big as a house.'

'Is it?' Catherine responded doubtfully. Be that as it may, she had the feeling that the door to that house was very firmly closed to her.

'Okay, let's have it.'

'Have what?'

'Catherine…' His sigh was very deep and pointedly patient. 'You aren't an easy lady to deal with; in fact on a count of one to ten you rate at something minus zero. I've asked myself more than once why I keep coming back for more.'

'Have you, indeed?' She drew herself up, aiming for a stately hauteur that would put him in his place—the effect of which was totally spoilt when he laughed out loud, causing her to flash back with, 'You needn't bother; you know that, don't you?'

'If only that was true.' There was undeniable amusement in his voice now which rankled even more. 'But somehow, somehow, you've got under my skin and there's nothing I can do about it. You turn me on, Catherine, but you're in here too.' He tapped his brow with a rueful hand. 'You drive me crazy at times, you test my patience to the limit, and I've never had so many cold showers in my life since you've come to the scene, but...I want you.'

'Keir—'

'But back to Martha and Bill.' He interrupted her panicky voice with a cool aplomb she envied. His words had aroused a sweet enchantment that was painful in its intensity, and she was alarmed at her vulnerability.

'Let me give you a little background history on them so you can understand better where Martha is coming from.'

'It doesn't matter—'

'It does to me.' This time she knew when to keep quiet, and she turned in her seat to watch his face as he talked. 'Martha and Bill were childhood sweethearts,' he said softly, 'crazy about each other from the cradle. They married when they were just nineteen, and both sets of families were from the farming community, but the top end of the market, so to speak. A lot of the farms round these parts were little more than smallholdings in those days, but their families were wealthy, very wealthy, and it looked as though their future was a rosy one when their wedding present was their own place. They had each other, two close and supportive families; they had it made in most folk's eyes.'

Hers too, Catherine thought with a fierce stab of envy that took her breath away.

'Martha had always wanted a big family,' Keir continued quietly, his eyes on the road ahead. 'But after a few months of marriage she had a miscarriage, followed by another six months later, then another, until the pattern was repeated year in and year out. They went everywhere, did everything, but still the miscarriages kept coming.

'Martha got desperate. It began to affect her mind and she wouldn't see anyone, shutting herself away on the farm and refusing all offers of comfort from friends and relations, until, twelve years on, the marriage was all but on the rocks. It can happen, you know…'

He turned to glance at her intent face with dark, narrowed eyes. 'You can home in on what's wrong, to the exclusion of everything else, until it becomes an obsession.'

He wasn't talking about Martha now, and they both knew it. But before Catherine could say anything he continued, 'Then she came to a crossroads when everything was at its worst, and the way she told it to my mother the choice was clear-cut—she could lose Bill, the farm, perhaps even her sanity, or she could look away from her own disappointment and pain and go with what she *had* been given rather than crying for the moon.'

'And so she did that, fell pregnant and everything was all right?' She didn't mean to sound cynical, but she had seen the photographs on the massive kitchen windowsill of Martha and Bill with their rosy-cheeked babies, little tots in school uniform, and later ones of smiling teenagers.

'Not exactly,' Keir said expressionlessly. They had been travelling along a fertile valley floor for some minutes, on a road that was little more than a rough dirt-track linking the farm to the outside world, and now he pulled in under a large, spreading elm tree and cut the engine, before climbing down and letting the dogs out from the back of the vehicle.

He walked round to her side of the Land Rover, where she was still sitting, and leant one muscled shoulder against the door, looking straight ahead down the valley as he talked through the open window.

'She began to talk to Bill, like she'd done in the years before the obsession got a hold, and they acknowledged they were wealthy, healthy, with a huge farmhouse that just begged for children but no foreseeable hope of ever filling it naturally.

'They decided to go in for the long-term fostering of problem kids—kids who had been through the mill one way or another—rather than adopting very young babies. Martha felt it was her way of making up for all the wasted years. They did that for several years, and then felt they wanted to do more, so they arranged with the social services to run a summer holiday home at the farm for under-privileged kids.'

'She hasn't any children of her own?' Catherine asked slowly.

'Not in the biological sense.' He was quite still, his arms folded across his chest and his voice even and almost without expression. 'They had six long-term foster children of their own, and then groups of other kids for a month or so through from May to September right up to a couple of years ago, when Bill suffered a mild heart attack. Of course their own foster children are often around—four live in the area and have kids of their own now—and many others come down for a visit on a regular basis to see their adopted mum and dad. They've straightened out a lot of lives in their own way.'

'And if they had had their own children none of that would have happened; that's what you're saying, isn't it?' Catherine said flatly. 'That it was the best thing—'

'No, that would be terribly presumptuous of me.' He put his hand through the open window, turning her face to meet his eyes. 'I'm sorry they didn't have the desire of their heart,' he said softly, 'but I admire them for playing the best they could with the cards they'd been dealt—*that* is what I'm saying, Catherine. Life isn't always fair; it can kick us so hard in the teeth that we think we'll never get up from under it, and some people don't. It makes them bitter, inward-looking; the chip on their shoulder becomes so heavy they're bowed down under the weight of it.'

She didn't want to hear this. She stared back at him, her shadowed eyes defensive and her chin jutting with painful defiance. She *had* to hold onto the consuming anger against the woman who had abandoned her—it was all she had. If she let go of that, if she allowed herself to feel any trace of longing, any hope that when she met her her mother might be glad to see her, even want her, she would become frighteningly vulnerable and exposed, and dangerously wide open to a last, final rejection.

This way she was safe. It would be *her* that would walk away with her head held high and her back straight. She wouldn't ask for anything, and she wouldn't expect it either. Not from her mother...and not from Keir.

She was grateful he hadn't believed Sandra's lies and she was touched by his faith in her, but she mustn't allow herself to run away with the idea that it meant more than it did. He was recovering from his wife's tragic death, a wife he had only had for a short time and whom he had, of course, loved—and Keir wasn't the sort of man to give his love easily.

Almost as though he had read her mind, he straightened, opening the door of the Land Rover and offering her his hand to alight. 'I want to talk to you, explain something, and it will be easier if we're walking,' he said flatly.

She stared at him for a moment as panic gripped her throat again, and then forced the feeling under control. 'All right.' But she didn't take his hand as she jumped down from the vehicle in one quick, light movement, thrusting her own hands deep in the pockets of her jeans and keeping her eyes on the gambolling dogs some fifty yards ahead.

Keir expelled a deep, silent breath. This wasn't going to be easy, but then he had never expected it to be. 'There's a stream down there among those trees; we'll walk the dogs that way and they can have a drink.' He glanced at her beautiful, pure profile with narrowed eyes. She looked scared to death, damn it, and it inspired such a mixture of emotions in him he had trouble distinguishing just one, except the frustration of continuously walking on egg shells. Enough was enough.

He didn't speak again until they reached the little copse of trees, and then his voice was magnificently matter-of-fact when he said, 'I wasn't in love with Marion when I married her.'

'What?' She couldn't believe she had heard right, her eyes huge as she stopped dead in her tracks and stared up into his dark, expressionless face.

'Not in the man-woman, romantic sense,' he continued evenly as though she hadn't spoken, taking her arm and forcing her to walk on at his side. 'There was a group of us at university, a few lads and girls, who got on well, were great mates, that sort of thing, with no physical intimacy clouding the friendships. We all had partners who came and went and were outside the circle, but it was an unwritten pact that we never moved in on each other—something we never discussed, but just knew.'

'And Marion was one of the girls?' she asked weakly. It was the last thing in the world she had expected him to say, and shock had numbed her reaction.

He nodded slowly. 'It was only the two of us out of the group who went to veterinary college but we continued to be there for each other, nothing heavy—or so I thought. But then Marion started to be ill all the time, one cold after another, that sort of thing. Looking back—' He stopped abruptly, shaking his head, his face drawn. 'Looking back I should have made her seek medical advice, but she just said she was low, that she'd get a tonic or something. A tonic!' His voice was tight and full of a raw self-contempt that caught at Catherine's heartstrings.

'Keir, it wasn't your fault; you didn't know.' She forgot all about self-protection and caution in her desire to comfort, catching hold of his arm as she spoke, her voice urgent. 'How could you have possibly guessed?'

He turned to face her, his eyes black with harsh self-condemnation. 'I should have known, Catherine; I was the only one who knew her that well. I knew she was terrified of medical people, hospitals, the whole caboodle. She had a phobia about it that was a result of an accident in her childhood, and it was like a ten-foot wall in her mind—unsurmountable. But I was working like mad, and she hid it so well—'

'You couldn't have known,' she said again, her voice soft and tender. 'You couldn't.' She was holding both of his arms now, the ridges of muscle hard beneath her fingers as she looked up into his face.

There was a long moment of silence as he gazed down at her, his body completely still but taut with tension, and then he took a deep, shuddering breath as he fought for control. 'We found out when she collapsed during one of the final examinations,' he said huskily, 'but by then it was too late—far too late. She felt so ill she thought she was going to die straight away, and so she told me—' He shook his head, his voice ragged. 'She told me that she loved me, that she'd always loved me, right from the first week of university years before.'

He turned away from her then, the movement harsh and abrupt, and stood with his back to her as he continued, 'But with the drugs they gave her she began to get better. Oh, we knew it was borrowed time. They were talking about nine months, twelve at the most, and probably a good proportion of those in hospital—which had the power to send her to hell and back every time she thought of it. Do you know what it's like to see someone you care about suffer like that?' he ground out grimly.

'No.' He had cared about Marion but he hadn't *loved* her. The thought was beating a tattoo in her head. Not in the way a man usually feels about the woman he marries.

'I pray you never will.'

'And so you married her,' she said quietly.

'And so I married her.' He turned to face her again. 'And it was a real marriage in every sense of the word,' he said evenly. 'Marion wanted it that way.'

It took more will-power than she had known she possessed to just nod quietly, the anguish that streaked through her soul at his admission shocking her with its intensity. Not that she resented Marion finding strength and peace in his arms to face the inevitable, she thought painfully; it wasn't that. It was the knowledge that if she could have swapped places with the tragic brunette, taken just a year of being his wife and having him close in exchange for the rest of her life, she would have done so.

'I'm sorry, Keir—for Marion, for you—'

'I didn't tell you for that.' His eyes were steady as he reached for her, holding her arms in much the same way she had held him a moment or two earlier, before pulling her closer to within a breath of his body, his face dark and handsome as he looked down into her troubled gaze. 'Do you have any idea how I feel about you?' he asked thickly. 'Any idea at all? I don't want to scare you off, I've told myself over and over that I've got to tread carefully, but damn it all, Catherine, I've never felt this way before, and it's killing me.'

'Keir, don't.' This was the ultimate irony in the snarled mess that made up her life, she thought desperately. She had known, even before the revelation about Marion, that what he felt was more than just a physical attraction. And it had terrified her; she had to admit it. It was the thing she had been fighting against every day she had been living under his roof, working with him, seeing him, loving him.

'I love you, Catherine.' The world went very still as

he said it, and for a moment everything was picked out in painful detail—the look on his face, the angle of his body, the trees behind and the blue sky above. 'I've never said that to any other woman—'

'No!' He didn't love her; she wouldn't believe it. This feeling he had for her might be more than just physical need but it wasn't love; she didn't, *couldn't* believe that. It would make the rest of her life too hard. Because she knew, suddenly and without the slightest measure of doubt, that she was too much of a coward to believe him. She couldn't believe he would continue to feel the same, for weeks, months, years. *She didn't trust him*; she didn't trust herself.

The mental abuse that she had suffered day in, day out from a tiny child right up to the moment she had walked out of the only home she had known for twenty-one years had savaged all the normal expectations—girlish dreams of a home and family, and settling down with one man who loved and adored her—clean away.

She knew that one day he would tell her it was over. She didn't know when, or how circumstances would unfold, but she would be waiting for that moment when she had been weighed in the balance yet again and found wanting. It had happened from the moment she could toddle, time and time again, and had eaten away at her self-perception and her confidence like a darkly insidious and avaricious black worm.

'Give me a child until he is seven and I'll have him for life'. The old phrase the Jesuits had used flashed into her mind. The woman she had called mother had had her for much longer than that…

'Catherine?' He gave her a gentle little shake, but his voice was tight when he said, 'This time I'm not going to allow you to escape and bring down the shutters, do you hear me? I don't care what's happened in your past—you could have been the worst sinner in the world before the day you came into my life and it won't affect how I feel. Your life started from the day I picked you up off that bench; that's what's real. And don't tell me you don't feel something for me because I won't believe it. And however little it is I'll build on that.'

'Stop this.' She wanted to scream and shout and wail with disgust at her own cowardice, tell him he didn't know her, that he didn't have a clue what she was really like, and that he'd run a mile if he did. But to do so would be to open the lid of Pandora's box, and she couldn't risk that. 'I don't want any sort of relationship with you or anyone else, Keir—'

'Yes, you do.' She had lowered her face as she spoke, and now he cupped her small jaw in his hand, forcing her tremulous gaze to meet his.

'No.' She shut her eyes, but still the glittering grey gaze was there in front of her closed eyelids, burning its way into her brain. 'It wouldn't work. Surely you see that?' she said desperately. 'We've only known each other a few weeks—'

'So we'll get to know each other better. I can be patient when I have to be.' She felt him take a deep breath. 'Open your eyes, Catherine. Look me full in the face and tell me you don't feel a thing for me,' he said softly, 'and then I promise I won't bother you again.'

She shook her head, keeping her eyes stubbornly closed.

'What are you so frightened of?' he asked huskily. 'That I might do this?' He kissed her slowly, and the thrill of sensation that shot through her tiny frame brought her jerking away from him, only to be pulled back into his hard body with a passion that told her his control was only skin-deep.

'You only have to tell me you don't want me,' he taunted gently. 'But properly, so I believe it.'

Her eyes were open now, the turmoil she was feeling reflected in their bruised blueness, but although she opened her mouth the words wouldn't come.

'I love you, Catherine,' he said again. 'I mean I *really* love you. I want you living with me, working with me, sharing the good times and the bad times, I want happy ever after—'

'There's no such thing,' she said weakly, forcing the words through the painful tightness in her throat.

'Yes, there is. I'll prove it; I'll give you a taste of it right now...' His hands cupped her face as his mouth took hers, the kiss hungry and possessive and frighteningly sweet, but although she could feel the fierce tension in his body, the control he was keeping on his desire, he was touching her gently, tenderly, as though she was something precious. And it was her undoing.

She kissed him back, straining into him as her love blanketed the fear and panic, and he froze for one infinitesimal moment before gathering her against him so closely she could feel the tremors sweeping through his muscled frame, and the pounding thud of his heart. How could she live in a world where he walked and talked and breathed, and yet be far from him? The thought seemed impossible as his hungry mouth stroked her tiny ears, moving on to the silky smoothness of her throat and neck, creating shivering rivulets of fire wherever it touched.

She was vaguely aware of the little inarticulate cries floating on the warm air, but ignorant of the fact that they came from her own lips, her whole being lost in a flood of sensation so strong, the rest of the world had ceased to exist. The hairy warmth of his skin, the muscled strength of his body, the wonder of what his mouth and hands were doing to her—they were the only real things in this world of colour and light and touch and taste into which she had plunged.

She was only conscious that they had slid down to the ground when the heady summer perfume of thick warm grass and wild flowers pervaded the sweetness. But then, as she felt the length of Keir's body against hers, it was all sensation again, his hard, male toughness fascinatingly at odds with the trembling of his body.

He kissed her slumberous eyelids, tasting their velvet silkiness with his tongue, before trailing feather-light, tantalising kisses to her mouth which was already open and waiting for his touch. He bit gently at her lower lip before teasing her tongue as he explored her mouth in an erotic arousal that turned her limbs liquid.

He was good, he was so, so good at this, she acknowledged faintly. But although the thought should have been a warning she couldn't respond to it.

Her hands were linked at the back of his muscled neck, and she could feel the silky bristles of his severe haircut as she ran her hands up into his hair. She loved him, she wanted him; she couldn't believe how much she wanted him...

'Now tell me again you don't believe in happy ever after,' Keir whispered huskily, his teeth nipping sensually at her ear. 'Tell me you don't believe I can make you happy. You're in my life, Catherine, like I'm in yours. There's no going back. Trust me; let me in.'

It was the one thing she knew herself to be incapable of. He felt her stiffen, her body freezing beneath his, and he couldn't believe she was doing it again—retreating into that formidable ivory tower and slamming the door shut.

He felt a hot surge of the rage and frustration he had felt on other occasions, but this time he didn't give her the space she silently demanded. He was *damned* if he was going to...

'If I wanted to I could take you right here and now and you know it,' he said grimly. 'If I cut the talking, did away with trying to find out what's going on in that head of yours—'

'Why don't you, then?' She tried to push him away, but the broad chest didn't move an inch, his muscles like iron. 'If you think it's that simple, why don't you?'

'Because I'm not an animal, Catherine, and I want more than your body.' He rolled away, sitting up in one swift movement and watching her with unfathomable eyes as she smoothed her clothing into place. 'I *will* have you. But it will be all of you, and not a hasty coupling in a field either. It will be slow and sweet, and you'll be there with me every inch of the way, mind, soul and body. It wasn't chance that brought you to Towerby. You might not be able to accept that right now, but it's the truth.'

He would never know the irony of those words. She raised her head and glanced across at him, and the pull of the sexual magic that pulsed from the big body was so tangible she could taste it on the air.

She had to end this now. She didn't quite know how things had gone so far, but if he ever guessed at his power over her she would be lost. She didn't *want* to love him, she didn't want to love anyone; love meant betrayal and pain and disillusionment, and she had had enough of that to last a lifetime.

She should never have come to Towerby. It had been a mission of revenge, and how could anything so flawed deserve to succeed anyway? She was no better than the woman who had brought her up in following through on this quest for retribution and reprisal against her natural mother. She didn't want to hurt anyone... The tears were stinging hot at the back of her eyes, but she dared not let them fall.

'It wasn't chance that brought me to Towerby,' she agreed dully. 'I planned to come here.'

The sudden elation he felt that she was going to open up to him was quenched by the look on her face and the deep desolation in her eyes. 'Catherine—'

As he made to move close to her again she jerked away so sharply he was immediately still, sensing she was at the very limit of her endurance.

'Some months ago I was ill with flu which developed

into pneumonia…' As she continued to talk, her voice flat and monotonous, he listened quietly, outwardly calm but inwardly burning with rage against the people who had so damaged the spirit of the woman in front of him. It took all of his considerable will power not to take her into his arms, but he knew now was not the time. She had to say it all first, open the wound and let the poison out.

'And you still have no idea who your real mother is?' he asked softly as she finished talking and shut her eyes, her body limp and drained. 'No clue at all?'

'No.' She shuddered at the tenderness in his deep voice. She had expected scorn at what she saw as her feebleness, disgust perhaps at her deceit, certainly a touch of self-righteous anger that she had been less than honest with him all the time she had lived under his roof. She could have coped with all those things, they didn't threaten her; she had lived with their twins all her life. But gentleness, consideration…they were dangerous— sweet little demons to undermine her resolve.

'Come here.' His voice was husky, deep with concern and desire, and her eyes shot open as her back straightened. She knew what she had to do now; she should have done it weeks ago.

'No, Keir.' It was difficult to look into the face she loved so much and say what she had to say, but she managed it—just. 'I've told you about my mother, my past life, so you'll understand my leaving has got nothing to do with you—'

'Leaving?' He didn't shout, but the tone of his voice made her stomach churn violently. 'You think I would let you leave?'

'You have no choice in the matter,' she said steadily, her voice firmer than it had been all day. 'You don't own me.'

'Yes, I do, in here.' He clenched a fist against his heart, the anger and frustration he was trying to conceal

narrowing his eyes into dark slits. He had never looked
more handsome, or more unattainable, she thought miserably, but she had to carry this through. He deserved
better than her. He needed an eager young wife, strong
in body and mind, to work alongside him and share the
load, make a family life, bear him children.

If, by some miracle, he didn't cast her aside once he
really got to know her, she would still be like a millstone
round his neck. She would never be able to live up to
his expectations and one day, *one day* those devastating
grey eyes would ice over, his heart would grow cold,
and she would have ruined his life as well as her own.

'I'm leaving, Keir.' She lifted her head proudly. 'I
mean it.' She stared at him, holding his gaze with her
own.

'What about your mother?' he said quietly.

'That doesn't matter any more.'

'You came all the way here, gave up your job, your
friends, and you say it doesn't matter?' he said tightly.
'That was only a few weeks ago—what the hell has happened to make you change your mind?'

You. 'It was stupid, a pipe-dream, to think I could find
her,' Catherine said wearily. 'And even if I could I realise now the only person I would hurt is myself. I might
cause her a few problems in the life she's made for herself, make her angry, embarrassed, but I couldn't bear—'
She stopped abruptly and then forced herself to go on.
'I couldn't bear to see her face when she looked at me.'

'She might be glad you'd found her,' Keir said softly,
the searing pain in her face gentling his voice. 'Have
you considered that?'

'She left me when I was a few weeks old, and she
hasn't been in touch once. She knew where I was; she
could have made contact at any time, but she didn't want
to.' She drew a shaking hand across her face. 'Those are
the facts.'

'And you hate her for that?'

'I don't know what I feel any more,' Catherine said huskily. 'I just know she's out there somewhere, somewhere close—I feel it in my bones—and she doesn't know me. I could walk past her in the street and I wouldn't know she was my mother. I keep looking at every woman about the right age, searching their faces, and the stupid thing is I don't even know what I'm looking for. I can't carry on like this,' she whispered painfully, her voice struggling. 'I don't want to.'

'If you run away now, you'll be running all your life. You know that, don't you?' he said grimly. 'Forget us for a moment; that aside I still think you should stay. I know people round here; I could make careful enquiries that your mother, if she's here, will never know about unless you want her to. I can help—'

'I don't want your help, Keir.' The well of loneliness that had always been a part of her, even from a tiny child, increased a few thousand feet. She steeled her heart as well as her voice, and said, 'You might think you love me, but you don't, not really. You don't know me. What you feel—'

'Don't tell me what I feel, Catherine.' He was angry and it showed, and when she would have taken a step backwards he caught her wrist, forcing her to remain still. 'I can accept you don't feel the same...yet,' he added deliberately, 'but give me the credit for knowing my own heart. I'm thirty years old, damn it, not some young teenager still wet behind the ears. I know what I want.'

'And I know what I want.' She stared at him, her eyes enormous in her white face, and lied like she'd never lied before. 'And it's not Towerby, or village life, or—'

'Me?' he finished grimly, dark colour flaring across his hard cheekbones.

'Or you.' She had to do this, make him hate her, or that tenacious streak in him would drag the truth out of her. 'I want a career in one of the big cities; the examinations I was working for when I became ill were to that end.' The touch of fact in the statement was enough to give a ring of genuineness to her words, and she saw the narrowed gaze flicker as he continued to search her face.

'I want my own flat, nice clothes; I don't want to have to be answerable to anyone other than myself.' If ever a picture filled her with horror it was the one she had just painted for herself. 'I want to see life, have fun.'

'I don't believe you.' He shook her slightly, the anger and frustration he was keeping under iron control causing his eyes to glitter and burn. 'I don't believe you're like that.'

'Like I said, you don't know me.' She dredged up a conciliatory smile from somewhere and forced herself to speak lightly. 'Of course, I shall always be grateful for all you've done for me, and I'm very honoured you want me to stay—'

'To hell with your gratitude.'

His eyes held hers for a moment more, and she was tempted, terribly tempted to fall against that muscled chest and tell him she loved him, adored him, that she'd do anything for him...

'Get in the Land Rover.' He had mastered the sudden explosion of rage. His voice was expressionless now, his face closed and cold, and once he had whistled to the dogs, and they were all safely in the back of the vehicle, he slid in beside her without saying a word, starting the engine immediately.

It was finished.

CHAPTER NINE

THE rest of the afternoon was a nightmare of endurance. Catherine and Keir visited two more large farms, neither of which was as prosperous or grand as the Alton premises, before driving right to the very top of Peak Fell to attend to a sick pig. The Robinsons' premises consisted of a small wind-blown farmhouse and several ramshackle outbuildings, and were situated in an exposed position where the grass was constantly flattened by the northern wind that blew with furious intent in the winter, a fact that the few spindly bent trees surrounding the buildings bore evidence to.

Keir hadn't said a word that wasn't absolutely necessary during the last hour and a half, and now, as he parked the Land Rover, he glanced at her briefly, his eyes remote and hooded. 'I won't be long.'

She had remained in the vehicle at the other two farms, but now something rebellious flared into life at the unspoken order that she stay put. 'Can I come?' she asked carefully. These were the sort of memories she was going to have to feed off for a long, long time once she was gone as she pictured him going about his daily work. 'I need to stretch my legs.'

His shrug was careless. He clearly didn't care one way or the other, and she really couldn't blame him, she thought miserably.

The patient was a huge sow with beady little eyes and wicked yellow teeth, but although she raised her head at Keir's entrance into her pen she made no effort to rise from her prone position. Keir's large hands were gentle but firm as he examined the animal, his manner reassuring to the anxious little smallholder who kept up a monologue of comforting baby talk to the pig whilst stroking the big, spiky head, in much the same way one would fuss over a pet dog or cat.

'She's going to be fine, Bob.' Keir smiled at the distraught man as he patted the sow's huge rump. 'She's got a touch of erysipelas; I'll give her an injection of serum right now, and you'll find that high temperature will rapidly come down. She'll be on her feet in twenty-four hours and ready to fight the world again.'

'Oh, I don't mind her bad temper,' the little man murmured equably. 'Me and Daisy understand each other, don't we, lass?' The mean little eyes glanced his way as one big ear flapped lazily, and Catherine couldn't help wondering what the smallholder saw in the animal to inspire him with such devotion. The pig was clearly more of a pet than a farm animal.

It was after five o'clock when they began the journey home, the late-afternoon sunlight highlighting the endless stone walls patterning the dales, and the gently dying heat of the day bringing the scents of thick moorland grass and wild flowers into the vehicle.

Had he believed her when she had outlined what she wanted for her future? Catherine asked herself painfully as she sat steeped in silent misery at Keir's side. She hoped she'd lied well. It would be fatal to let him guess that her heart and soul would always be here, that she would never stop aching for what might have been if things had been different, if *she'd* been different.

The long garden was gently dozing in the warmth as Keir opened the gate and stood aside to let her pass through, his big body distant and remote, his face closed. One wall was covered with pale yellow velvet-petalled rambling roses in full bloom, and the thought came that she would never be able to smell that rich, heavy perfume again without experiencing the grinding anguish she was feeling now.

Keir went straight into the surgery after leaving the dogs in the garden with bowls of cold water, and as Catherine climbed the stairs to the flat she found her head was pounding, the events of the traumatic day having given her a thudding headache. She would have a bath and stay in her room tonight, she thought wearily as she opened the front door to the flat, and then tomorrow she would pack and leave whilst the morning surgery was in progress. Keir had Martin and Mary Napier now—even her usefulness was finished.

'Thank goodness you're back!' Janice leapt out of her room as she heard Catherine's key in the lock. 'You'll never guess what I've done. Is Keir with you?' she added anxiously, glancing behind Catherine. 'I need to talk to him too.'

'He's downstairs.' Catherine tried to muster some enthusiasm in her voice as she asked, 'What's the matter?'

'I'd forgotten, I'd *totally* forgotten that Michael's mother has invited us all over for a meal tonight,' Janice said agitatedly, running her hand through her dark hair so it stuck out in every direction. 'She mentioned it a week ago and I meant to clear it with you and Keir, but I just forgot. And then when Michael reminded me today I didn't have the nerve to say I hadn't told you, especially when she's got everything in. He's always moaning I'm not organised enough, and we've already had one row on the subject lately when I double-booked us at the weekend, if you remember?'

Catherine did remember. Janice and Michael had gone to dinner with some newly married friends when another couple had arrived at the flat to take them out for a drink. As it was the third time in as many weeks that Janice had done something similar Michael had been less than pleased, and things had got pretty heated for a time, until

Janice had promised faithfully she would write everything down in her diary in future.

'You aren't doing anything, are you?' Janice asked
anxiously. 'Please say you aren't.'

What could she say? Catherine stared at the other girl
as she understood, for the first time, how Janice's hap-
hazard approach to life could so infuriate Keir and
Michael. How could she possibly endure an evening in
Keir's company after everything that had happened that
afternoon? It would be hell on earth for them both, and
all because Janice had forgotten to mention Michael's
mother's invitation. But she would have to go; it would
place Janice in an impossible situation with Michael
again if she didn't.

'No, I'm not doing anything, Janice,' she said quietly,
her headache intensifying at the thought of the evening
ahead. 'But I don't suppose Keir can drop everything
without any warning; there's a couple of new patients
from this morning in the recovery room that need careful
monitoring. I'm quite happy to come with you and
Michael, though, if Keir can't make it.'

'Perhaps Martin would stand in?' Janice suggested
hopefully. 'If not I'll have to say there was some sort of
emergency, but I bet Michael will guess the truth. He
knows me too well.'

Say you can't come, Keir, say you can't come.
Catherine continued to send silent signals all the time
Janice was downstairs, but when the other girl popped
her head round Catherine's door a few minutes later her
smiling face told its own story.

'No problem,' she beamed happily. 'I got another lec-
ture, but Keir could see it wasn't fair on Michael's mum
not to come. You'll love her, Catherine, she's such a
pet.'

'Is she?' Catherine stopped listening as the other girl
prattled on. Well, this was certainly going to be an eve-

ning to remember, for Keir as well as her! She still couldn't believe what he felt for her was love—how could a man like Keir love *her*?—but whatever it was she had caused him embarrassment and pain, hurt his pride and dented his male ego.

Oh... She came to herself again to find she was alone, Janice having left to get ready. How could she bear it? How could she leave and never see him again? The thought made her feel physically sick, and for long, searing minutes she took great lungfuls of air, willing the nausea to subside.

And if she left this place she would never see her mother. She knew it, just as she knew she was close somehow. It wasn't a knowledge born of logic, but it was as hard as concrete, a sixth sense that had been awakened by something outside herself. And she wanted to see her...

She walked across to the door and shut it very quietly, before flinging herself down on the bed and crying as though her heart would break. Just once, *just once* she wanted to look into the face of the woman who had given birth to her, to see what her own flesh and blood looked like, to hear her speak. And it wasn't because she hated her, or wanted to spoil her life—nothing like that. She brought her hands across her chest as the pain became too much to bear. Perhaps it never had been. She just wanted to know if there was any chance that her mother had regretted what she'd done, had thought about her sometimes, wished she could see her...

'Oh, God, help me.' She groaned the words through such an anguish of soul that it had her screwing herself up into a tight little ball, the pain unbearable. 'Do something, show me; I can't go on...' She had made such a mess of everything; it had all gone from bad to worse like a runaway train that was out of control. And now she had hurt Keir, and she had to spend a whole evening pretending to be someone else, someone who had their heart set on a career and the high life.

She continued to pray, in fits and starts, for some time, her thoughts spiralling round and round like a huge roller coaster, until gradually she became quiet, a sense of peace pervading her troubled mind and blanketing her soul.

'How could someone do that to a little baby?' She spoke out loud into the quiet room, rising off the bed and walking across to the window, her eyelids heavy with weeping. She felt so sorry for the little baby she had been, but this time when she thought of it there was none of the bitter anger that had coloured such thoughts before, just a deep sense of sorrow and regret.

She didn't understand, she thought sadly, her eyes following a lone bird as it soared in the sky outside, its wings making good use of the warm air currents. And perhaps she never would. But if she was ever going to build some sort of a life for herself, learn to fly above the misery and despair of her early years and soar in the warm air currents of life, she had to let go of the crippling resentment and rage, justified though such emotions were.

Perhaps that was why she had been guided here? She continued to watch the carefree bird in the light-washed sky as dusk slowly put fingers of pink and mauve into the scene outside the window, other birds joining the first one as they feasted on insects the warm evening had brought out. Perhaps she had never been meant to find her mother. Maybe she'd had it all wrong from the beginning.

She was ready when Janice knocked on her door at eight, her careful use of cosmetics hiding the utter exhaustion that seemed to have taken her over. As she joined the others in the hall she felt as though she was in some kind of vacuum, a suspended void in the gallop of time that was surreal, dream-like.

The strange serenity took something of a knock when she looked at Keir. He seemed to fill the light-coloured hall, the black trousers and charcoal-grey shirt he was wearing making him seem even bigger than usual, the muscled strength of his powerful shoulders and chest very evident under the dark material.

He looked back at her, the sharply defined angles of his face hard and handsome and his stone-grey eyes expressionless as they took in the small, slim woman in front of him, dressed simply in an ankle-length full-skirted dress in white cotton, the plain colour relieved by a vivid violet-coloured belt that exactly matched the colour of her eyes.

'You look very lovely.' Catherine couldn't quite determine the tone of his voice, but she was aware of Janice's gaze darting between them, and then, as the moment stretched and became painful, she tore her eyes from his.

'Thank you.' He could have been carved in granite, she thought helplessly; she couldn't read a thing from his sombre face. 'So do you—look nice, that is,' she added hastily as her cheeks began to flame. 'And you, Janice.' She managed a quick smile at Keir's sister who still hadn't said a word.

'We'll bring the mutual admiration society to a close and get moving, shall we?' Keir drawled lazily. 'Mustn't let Michael's parents think we've forgotten, eh, Janice?'

It was below the belt, but in the circumstances all Janice could do was smile sweetly, although she obviously found it painful. 'Keir, you won't… You won't let on…?'

'My lips are sealed.' He glanced across at Catherine, the devastating grey gaze lingering on her mouth. 'How about yours?'

'I... Yes—I won't say a word, Janice.'

He was doing this on purpose, Catherine thought tightly as she followed Janice out of the flat, sailing past Keir with her nose in the air—the effect of which was spoilt by the brilliant colour staining her cheeks. He was trying to make her feel uncomfortable, embarrassed, because of this afternoon. *This afternoon...* The memory of how it had felt to be crushed close to that big, male frame suddenly obliterated the last of her fatigue, producing a rush of adrenaline that was more effective than any number of black coffees.

Well, she would get through this evening without rising to his subtle bait, and once they were in the car driving home, with Janice as chaperon, she would tell him that she was leaving in the morning. She ignored the savage thud her heart gave, and concentrated on putting one foot in front of the other as she walked down the stairs, acutely aware of Keir just behind her when she reached the bottom.

'This way.' As both women made to walk along the passage to the back of the house Keir unlocked the front door, before calling through into the reception area, 'Martin? We're off now. See you later, and thanks for holding the fort at such short notice.'

'My pleasure.' Martin's voice drifted through from the other room. 'Have a nice time.'

'A taxi?' Janice stood still on the top of the steps as she stared at the taxi-cab waiting in the street outside.

'Well spotted.'

'But we don't usually have a taxi.' Janice obviously didn't appreciate the brotherly sarcasm, as her terse tone made clear.

'Perhaps I'm trying to convince Catherine that we aren't quite the heathens we appear to be, and that even in the deep, dark wilds of Yorkshire we have the refinements of modern living,' Keir said pleasantly but with lethal intent. 'Besides which, I've found that Ian's taste in wine isn't to be frowned at, and I'm rather in need of some fortification tonight.'

'Oh.' Janice had clicked on to the fact that all was not well. 'Bad day?' she asked carefully.

'I've had better.'

Michael's parents lived on the outskirts of the next village, which was a bare five miles away, but, seated next to Keir in the back of the taxi, his hard thigh pressed close to hers and his arm stretched along the back of the seat in a manner that looked casual but which she just knew was meant to keep her fully aware of him, it seemed like fifty.

Dusky golden sunlight was slanting onto the roof of the beautiful thatched cottage when the taxi nosed its way through wrought-iron gates and onto a large rectangle of pebbled drive surrounded by a big, riotous border of boisterously unrestrained flowers. Hollyhocks, lupins, blue larkspur, brilliant scarlet snapdragons, the trumpet-shaped fragrant pink and white flowers of naked lady, Michaelmas daisies, clusters of lavender-blue Queen Anne's lace and feathery white baby's-breath all jostled for space, along with candytuft, lovely white anemones and the brilliant gold of faithful little marigolds.

It was breathtaking, an English garden at its best, and Catherine stood for a long moment in the dying sun once she was out of the car, breathing in the rich perfume of a host of gillyflowers as the peace she had felt earlier stole over her again.

'A little touch of English village life for you to see.' Keir's voice was deep and soft behind her, and when his hand closed over her bare elbow she felt the contact right down to her toes. 'If we can provide the fun too that's half of your criteria for a successful evening met.' His tone was sardonic as it stated he hadn't forgotten her words from the afternoon, and as she spun round to face him her face tightened.

'That's uncalled for—' she began furiously, only to stop abruptly when he placed a warning finger on her lips as Janice joined them.

'Look, is anything wrong?' Janice was clearly out of her depth as her eyes moved from Keir's mocking face to Catherine's angry one. 'I'm sorry I sprang this on you tonight—'

'No problem.' The taxi had swung round in a semi-circle, and just as it left the heavy oak door to the cottage swung open. 'And here's your beloved, right on cue,' Keir continued easily, raising his hand to Michael who was standing in the doorway, with an older couple just behind him.

'What *is* the matter?' Janice asked testily as they walked towards the others, but there was no time to answer as Michael stepped forward, his face wreathed in a smile of welcome, and introductions commenced.

'Catherine, these are my parents.' He stepped to one side as he waved at the couple behind him. 'My mother—another Catherine, I'm afraid, so forgive any confusion tonight—and my father, Ian.'

'How do you do?' Catherine smiled politely, but it was an effort. Whether it was due to the fact that Keir's hand had now snaked round her waist and she had been drawn very firmly into his side, or that Michael's mother wasn't at all what she had expected, she wasn't sure. She was very small—her doctor husband towered over her by a good nine inches—but it was her face that had arrested Catherine.

She knew Michael was the same age as Keir—thirty—and she had expected his parents to be around the fifty mark, probably going grey, but tanned and robust like most of the people hereabouts. But his mother was tiny—ethereal was the word—and although her face still bore evidence of what must have been great beauty in her youth her hair was pure white, utterly devoid of colour.

How old was she? Catherine found she could hardly tear her eyes away from the other woman's face. She could be any age from forty to sixty, her skin still fine and translucent, but the web of lines radiating from her eyes and mouth and the deep sadness in her eyes suggesting a tragedy in her past that had ravaged her beauty almost cruelly. It was a gentle face, a tragic face, and Catherine felt herself drawn to it without knowing why.

'Catherine, please come in...' Michael's mother made a little fluttering gesture with her hand that suggested nervousness, and as Catherine felt Keir's arm tighten round her body she glanced up into his face and saw he was looking at the other woman with something akin to shock darkening his eyes.

'Keir?' As they followed the others into the cottage—a vision of olde-world charm—he seemed determined not to let go of her. 'What's the matter?'

'It's not possible.' He was talking as though to himself, but with his eyes on her face. 'Catherine, you said your mother's name was Anna—Anna Mitchell?' he asked urgently.

She nodded, frightened by the expression on his face.

'Then how—?' His murmur was cut short as they joined the others in the beautiful little Victorian summer house attached to the dining room at the back of the house, where a trolley of drinks was waiting.

There was a strange atmosphere prevailing as everyone was settled in big, comfy cane chairs with their drinks. Ian kept very close to his wife, his eyes constantly darting to her face, which was as white as lint, and even Michael seemed to sense that something was wrong, his glances at his parents troubled as he mixed and deposited drinks, and offered round the little tray of hors d'oeuvres.

'Michael tells us you live in London, Catherine.' It was a relief when Michael's mother engaged her in conversation—even the normal banter between Michael and Janice had been stilted and forced. 'You're down here on holiday, I understand?' she asked gently. 'Recuperating after an illness?'

'Yes, in a way.' She had already told Keir, so there was no point in perpetuating the lie. 'I've actually left London, and I'm having a break before I move on to Birmingham to live and work.' One city was as good as another, and she had decided on Birmingham that afternoon as she had watched Keir come and go about the farms.

She felt him stiffen at her side on the small cane sofa for two where he had deftly sat them, but he said nothing, and she didn't dare look at his face.

'You've family in London?' It was a perfectly reasonable question, but the look on Michael's mother's face was making Catherine feel uncomfortable.

How did she answer that? She had no family in London—the people who had brought her up had never been a family to her—but polite pre-dinner conversation didn't lend itself to the truth. 'I'm adopted.' She saw the words register in the other woman's eyes like a blow. 'And my adoptive family and I don't get on, so I don't really have any ties there, if that's what you mean.'

Her heart was beginning to pound, and the feeling that she had met this woman before, that she knew her in some way, was growing. But there was a chilling numbness holding part of her brain, the part that had hoped and prayed and groaned for the last few months since she had found out the truth about herself.

'What's your surname?' As Ian moved to put his arm round his wife's shoulders, she was aware of Keir doing exactly the same to her, but the icy trickles that were shivering down her spine were holding her transfixed.

She stared at the woman in front of her, utterly unable to speak, her heightened senses taking in Michael and Janice in one part of the room—clearly bewildered by what was happening, as their unnatural stillness showed—the evening bird-song beyond the open door of the summer house where the large garden stretched, the blue sky through the windows, the shadow falling across her mother's face... *Her mother's face.*

'Prentice.' It was a whisper.

'And you are twenty-one years old, and you have a tiny birthmark on your thigh in the shape of the moon... Catherine, oh, Catherine...'

'You're my mother.'

'And you're my baby, my precious, precious baby.' How she came to be clasped in her mother's arms she wasn't sure; her eyes were blinded by tears, but the arms holding her were strong for all their fragility, and the embrace was soft and warm and perfumed, and went on and on.

She was aware of muted hustling and bustling at the sides of them, but she was incapable of pulling herself together for long minutes, and when eventually she did raise her head it was to see her mother sitting beside her on the sofa—and she realised they were quite alone. Her mother's face—the face she recognised was so like hers now she knew—was drenched in tears, but lit with an inner light that told her all she wanted to know.

'You don't mind that I've found you?' Catherine whispered brokenly. 'I thought...'

'Mind?' Her mother shut her eyes for a second and her face crumpled as she said, 'I've lived for this moment for twenty-one years—dreamed it, breathed it. Without believing that one day we would be reunited I wouldn't have remained sane.'

'But why——?' Catherine stopped abruptly.

'Why, feeling like that, did I give you up?' her mother said softly. 'Can I tell you, explain from the beginning? It won't excuse what I did—nothing can do that—but if you just understand how it was...'

Catherine nodded without speaking, her mind still stunned by the enormity of it all, and her mother gathered her close for one minute more, as though she couldn't bear to let her go, before drawing away and composing her face, which was awash with tears again.

'I was very confused when I met the young man who was your father—confused, lonely and unhappy. I was just seventeen, my parents had been killed in a horrific accident I'd witnessed, and the effect on me was very traumatic. My sister, my adopted sister, was already married and I'd been placed with her. We didn't get on, but I knew lots of siblings who were the same, and she was the only family I'd got. But she treated me badly, and when I met Alan...'

Her voice trailed away, and she took a deep breath before she continued, 'When I met Alan I fell for him hook, line and sinker. He...he told me he loved me, that he'd look after me, that we'd get married and I could leave my sister's home, and then...then I got pregnant.'

She raised her head and looked Catherine full in the face. 'He left the same week,' she said bleakly. 'My parents had always been very protective, and I was painfully naive for my age—not that that excuses anything. I was offered an abortion but I couldn't, I just couldn't, and so I continued with the pregnancy although my sister made each day an ordeal.

'But, when I saw you, it was all worth it. You were so beautiful, so perfect; I loved you instantly. I named you Catherine Joy—Catherine because that's my second name and Joy—because of the joy I felt when I first saw you and knew you were mine.'

'And then?' Catherine found she was holding her mother's hands in her own. 'What then?'

'It was a hard birth, and I was ill—physically and mentally—afterwards. I brought you home and all my sister did was go on at me—that I was unfair, how you would suffer without a father, the cruelty other children would subject you to, the things I was depriving you of—on and on and on. She said she could give you everything and I could give you nothing, and in the end I cracked. I became very ill in my mind.'

She shook her head blindly. 'The loss of my parents, Alan's desertion, the pregnancy and the birth, and then the pressure from her afterwards—it was just too much, I suppose. And so I gave in. She couldn't have children, and she wanted you so much. I knew with them you would have a normal family life, that they could give you everything I couldn't.'

Oh, the irony of it all. Catherine looked at the pain-ravaged face in front of her and knew she couldn't tell her the truth—not now, perhaps not ever. There were some things love had to carry.

'My sister was adamant I couldn't see you again, that it had to be a complete severance or else she wouldn't feel you were hers. I could understand that, in a way, but it was the hardest thing of all. If I could just have stayed on the perimeter of your life, seen you occasionally...'

'And so you came to Yorkshire,' Catherine said gently, the knowledge that her mother had suffered even more than she had through the years wrenching her heart in a way she would have considered impossible just days—hours—ago.

'I came as housekeeper to Ian after answering an advertisement.' Her mother brushed a wisp of white hair from her brow with a trembling hand. 'I told my sister where I was, that if at any time—*any time*—in the future

she would let me see you I would come straight there...
But I knew she wouldn't. My one hope through the years
was that you would try and find me when you were old
enough to do so.'

'And you married Ian?' Catherine asked quietly. And
became Michael's mother. It hurt; she couldn't help it.

'When I came up here I was on the verge of a nervous
breakdown, and leaving you tipped me over the edge.
Ian was so good; instead of me being housekeeper to a
nine-year-old boy and his father, they looked after me
for months and months until I began to recover. I told
Ian everything; he's a very good man.'

Her mother shook her head slowly. 'He asked me to
marry him twelve months later, and he understood I
could never give him a child. I felt that to do so would
be a betrayal of you in some way, and he accepted that.
Michael loves me, as I do him, but perhaps because of
my illness in the early days it was not the traditional
mother/son relationship. He is very protective, but looks
on me more as an older sister, I think. And you—you
are my only child, Catherine, my precious only child.'

She reached out a shaky hand and touched Catherine's
face. 'I've looked at your photo every day we've been
apart.'

'Did you know, when you asked me here tonight?'
Catherine asked quietly, her heart thudding when she
realised how easily she could have missed it. 'Did you
know I was your daughter?'

'I wasn't sure. Janice had mentioned you, of course,
and the name, the age, the fact you were from London
all seemed right. But she said you were on holiday—'

'I wasn't. I came looking for you,' Catherine said
quickly. 'But for Anna—Anna Mitchell.'

'I used my second name when I came here—it was
the only link I had left with you—and then of course I
married Ian so my surname changed...' She stopped and

they both looked at each other for a long moment, the wonder of it all reflected in both faces. 'I thought you might hate me for giving you away,' her mother said softly with a little catch in her voice, her eyes expressing far more than the words said.

'I love you,' Catherine said just as softly. 'You're my mum.'

CHAPTER TEN

'CAN'T sleep?'

Keir's voice was soft and deep, but Catherine still nearly jumped out of her skin as he came up behind her in the dark lounge. It had been two in the morning before they had got back to the flat, after an evening containing so much gruelling emotion, Catherine had thought she would fall asleep on her feet. But once alone in her room she'd found her mind was buzzing with a thousand images, a thousand words, a thousand fragmented scenarios, and try as she might she couldn't stop pacing the floor.

At four she had given up any notion of sleep, opening her door quietly and padding out into the hall in just her nightie and towelling robe to make herself a cup of coffee in the silent kitchen.

Once in her favourite seat in the shadowed lounge—in a big easy chair overlooking the sleeping village below—she had curled her feet beneath her, and with her hands cradling the coffee mug had allowed her thoughts to roam at will.

She had found her mother, and never in her wildest dreams had she allowed herself to imagine she would be loved, wanted, *needed* so very much. Ian had taken her aside at one point during the evening to tell her, quietly and very gently, that he believed the crucifying grief his wife had felt over leaving her daughter behind had turned her hair white when she had come to Yorkshire. 'There hasn't been a day since I've known her that she hasn't spoken your name,' he'd said softly, his arm round her shoulders. 'I can't tell you what it means to

both of us to have you here, Catherine. We've prayed
for this day for twenty-one years.'

Yes, there was no doubt that she was loved and
wanted, that the doors to her mother's heart and her
home were wide open. So why, when everything had
turned out so incredibly, so miraculously well, did she
feel as though she had missed something somewhere?
Since she had prayed yesterday evening she'd felt she
was being shown something, but she hadn't grasped it,
and the feeling was even more urgent now, since she
had found her mother.

She turned in the chair now to look up at Keir, and
her heart gave a giant lurch at the sight of him, big and
dark, just behind her. He was still in the clothes he had
worn earlier in the evening, and she said the first thing
that came into her mind. 'Haven't you been to bed?'

'No.' He walked in front of her, settling one thigh on
the broad windowsill as he looked back at her, the bright
moonlight making the room a stark contrast of clear
shapes and dark shadows. 'I've been in the garden since
we got back...thinking.'

'Oh.' She hardly dared breathe.

'Do you know what about?' he asked softly, the expression on his face making her heart thud still harder
and her mouth go dry.

She had to lick her lips before she could speak, and
his narrowed gaze followed the action, the sensual gleam
in his eyes making her hot. 'No.'

'You. You, my hard-hearted little sprite.'

'I'm not hard-hearted!'

Her very real indignation caused his mouth to curve
in a wry, crooked smile. 'No?' He let his gaze run over
her face, her eyes, her lips, her throat, and she felt its
impact as though he were actually caressing her, her skin
growing pink and her breathing quickening.

'I don't have to touch you, do I? I don't even have to

touch you and you melt for me,' he said thickly. 'And you're talking about leaving here.'

'That's just sex.'

'The hell it is.' He glared at her before shaking his head and saying more softly, 'The hell it is. I love you, Catherine. I love you more than I ever imagined loving a woman, and there is no way I'm going to let you walk out of my life.'

'Keir—'

'No, cut the "Keir"s and the "I can't"'s,' he growled slowly. 'I'm not being kept at arm's length by them any more. I know you, Catherine; I know you in here.' He thumped the front of his chest angrily. 'I know the sort of woman you are, and there is no way you would respond to me like you do unless you felt something for me beyond the desire for a quick tumble in bed.

'And I'll tell you quite frankly—' a touch of chagrin entered the grim voice for a moment '—if I hadn't needed more from you than an easing of my body you'd have been bedded weeks ago. Because I *want* you, Catherine; physically I want you very much indeed. The things I imagine doing to you—' The twist of his mouth expressed dark self-derision. 'Believe me, you would be in no doubt that I want you.'

She loved him, oh, she loved him, but she didn't dare believe what he felt for her would last. Something of what she was feeling must have been written on her face, because he reached out for her, pulling her up and into his arms before she could move. 'I'm not letting you go, Catherine; get that into your head first of all,' he said in a smoky, thick voice that made her quiver. 'If you leave here I'll find you and bring you back; it's as simple as that. Besides which, you have family here now; you can't escape me.'

She didn't want to; there was nothing she wanted less. 'It wouldn't work.' She pushed against his broad chest, feeling the thud of his heart against her hand and realising he wasn't as calm as he was acting.

'The only way you can convince me of that is to say you feel nothing for me,' he stated softly. 'Me as a person. Tell me, Catherine—tell me I just turn you on, that there is nothing else there at all, and if I believe you I'll leave you alone. I promise you that.'

'Keir, this is ridiculous—'

'Tell me. Tell me you just want fun with no emotional ties, that you are hell-bent on climbing that career ladder to the exclusion of any personal commitment. I wouldn't stop you having a career if that was what you wanted, Catherine.'

He took her face between his big hands, the grey eyes that could appear so cold glowing like sun-warmed stone. 'Of course I want a family, children, one day. But it can be years from now, decades, if that's what you want—'

'It's not my career. Don't you *see*? It's me.' The words were torn out of her, the emotional roller coaster of the last few hours breaking down all her defences. Fear was like a thick mist, choking her, strangling her, panic at her own inadequacy so real she could taste it, bitter and tart, on her tongue. 'I can't be what you want, Keir. It would all go wrong and you...you'd be disappointed.'

'What are you talking about?' He stared at her with very real amazement on his face. 'Is it something that's happened in your past? Is that it? I don't care; I told you when you met me the slate was wiped clean.'

'It's not anything that's happened—not in that way. I told you everything yesterday. I've never...I've never gone with a man. It's just that you could have anyone,' she whispered dully.

'But the one I want is a silver-haired girl with eyes I

could drown in,' he said softly. 'I don't want anyone else; I never will.'

'You think that *now*—'

'Catherine, what do you want from me?' His hands moved to her shoulders and he shook her gently. 'I'm turning myself inside out here—'

'But that's part of it, don't you understand?' she said urgently, jerking away from him and shaking her head wildly. 'You want someone uncomplicated, easy to be with, someone who can make you happy.'

'Stop playing the martyr!' The words, and the tone he used, were like a bucket of cold water over her head, and she froze in shock, her eyes enormous as she stared into his angry face, before stepping forward and hitting him once, very hard, across the face.

'How dare you? How dare you say that to me?' she spat furiously . 'I hate you—'

'No, you don't, you love me.' He had both her wrists in one hand now, his other arm moving her struggling body against his, where she continued to twist and turn, her breath sobbing in her throat. 'And I love you, and I'm not going to let you throw away the one chance of happiness we both have because of what's happened in your past. I could kill your family for what they've done to you, but they are your past and I'm your future; do you hear me?

'When I saw you next to your mother yesterday I could've kicked myself for not realising who she was before, but when I've looked at Ian's wife in the past all I've seen is a sad, tragic figure who has always been something of a recluse.'

She had stopped struggling now, and he put her to arm's length whilst keeping hold of her shoulders. 'I'm not going to let that happen to you, Catherine, however much you fight me. Together we are going to beat this thing; you are not going to let that maniac who brought you up wreck your life too. I can't promise you I'll always be the perfect husband. I'm human; I make mistakes—I get too wrapped up in my work and take too much on, I'm untidy, I leave the top off the toothpaste. But one thing I can promise you...'

He paused, pulling her against him and holding her face with his hand. 'I'll always love you, always be there for you, always need and want you, till death and beyond.'

She hadn't realised she was crying, silently, until he bent forward and took her salty lips in a long, deep kiss as his hands moved over her body in an intimate caress.

'We are going to build our *own* life, with our *own* family, and you'll learn to believe it—I promise you that too,' he said shakily after long, sweet minutes of lovemaking. 'You'll see your children playing with their grandmother and you'll heal her mind too, give her back the years that the locust has eaten. It *will* happen, Catherine, I promise you.'

'All these promises...' She tried to smile, but the tears flowed again.

'But first you have to say you love me; you never have, you know,' he said huskily, and just for a moment she saw a flash of uncertainty, of a desperate need for reassurance in the face of this big, controlled, authoritative man she loved so much, and it melted the last of her resistance.

'I do—I do so much—but I can't help being frightened...'

'That's fine.' He held her so tightly she thought her ribs would crack. 'I can deal with that. I've got all the time in the world, the rest of our lives, to convince you of how much you're loved.'

It was said with such arrogance—that same arrogance

that had so got under her skin when they had first met—that she wanted to smile, but he had captured her mouth again and her soul was flying.

EPILOGUE

THE only place they could have considered being married was the ancient little thirteenth-century parish church in the middle of Towerby, and it seemed to Catherine that the whole of the village had turned out as she walked up the long, winding path to the church door on Ian's arm.

Keir had wanted a December wedding, telling her that the best Christmas present in the world would be to wake up beside her on Christmas Day. And Mother Nature had conspired to add her own touch of magic to the occasion, draping the trees and hedgerows with a brilliant, glittering mantle of frost beneath a clear winter sky of deep cloudless blue, creating a white, diamond-studded wonderland.

'All right?' As they reached the top of the path and Catherine turned round to smile at Janice behind her, resplendent in her bridesmaid's regalia of wine and ivory, Ian's quiet voice at her side brought her eyes snapping back to his.

'I think so,' she said shakily.

The girl in the mirror who had stared back at her just a few minutes before leaving her mother's house hadn't looked familiar, the frothy satin and lace ivory dress and fur-lined cape and hood edged in wine silk giving her an ethereal beauty that was quite breathtaking and a little awe-inspiring, her skin a delicate, translucent cream and her hair like spun silver.

'I think he's waiting.' Ian smiled at her, and she felt a surge of love for this quiet man who had been a tower of strength to her mother since the day they had met,

185

and who had accepted her into his family as his own daughter without a second thought, becoming the father she had never had as easily as if she were his natural child.

As the strains of the Bridal March began Catherine felt a little fluttering of panic, and then she was walking through the small arched doorway, Ian's comforting bulk at her side, and beginning the walk up the aisle. Every pillar, every windowsill of the beautiful old church was festooned with flowers, their fragrance filling the building. But she only had eyes for the tall, dark man standing with Michael in front of the altar.

Would she make him happy? Could she forget the past and reach out to the future? And then he turned, while she was still a few feet away, and smiled at her, and she knew she had nothing to prove to Keir, and never would have. He loved her; he loved her more than she had imagined herself ever being loved.

His parents were smiling at her on her right, a bevy of uncles and aunts beaming their approval in the seats behind, and then she caught sight of her mother's face in the pew opposite, her eyes sparkling with tears of joy and happiness and her face alight with love.

She was covered in love, deluged with it, wrapped in its delicious warmth as she floated to Keir's side and Ian placed her hand in his, Michael grinning at her from Keir's other side.

'A few minutes more and you're really mine.' Keir's voice was low and deep, and for her ears only.

'I'm yours.' She smiled at him, her tears of happiness glittering like diamonds in the deep blue of her eyes. 'I've always been yours.' She was home.

Jayne Ann Krentz

Lady's Choice

Travis Sawyer has a plan for revenge. Juliana Grant has a
plan too—she has picked Travis as Mr Right. When
Travis takes over the resort in which Juliana has invested
her money, Juliana takes matters
into her own hands.

*"Jayne Ann Krentz is one of the hottest writers
in romance today."*—USA Today

1-55166-270-1
AVAILABLE FROM MARCH 1998

Catherine Coulter

Afterglow

Chalk-and-cheese lovers Chelsea Lattimer and
David Winter finally find happiness after a series
of disastrous relationships—thanks to their
match-making friends.

Afterglow is a wonderful romantic comedy from
New York Times bestselling author Catherine Coulter.

1-55166-472-0
AVAILABLE FROM MARCH 1998

JANICE KAISER

FAIR GAME

Dana Kirk is a rich and successful woman, but someone
wants to kill her and her teenage daughter. Who hates
her enough to terrorise this single mother? Detective
Mitchell Cross knows she needs help—
his help—to stay alive.

*"...enough plot twists and turns to delight
armchair sleuths"*—Publishers Weekly

1-55166-065-2
AVAILABLE FROM MARCH 1998

MIRA®

SANDRA BROWN

THE THRILL OF VICTORY

Stevie Corbett's life is on the line, but her fate rides on
keeping the truth a secret. Judd Mackie's job is
to uncover secrets. After dogging Stevie for
years, Judd now has the story of the year.
All he has to do is betray her trust.

"One of fiction's brightest stars!"
—Dallas Morning News

1-55166-025-3
AVAILABLE FROM FEBRUARY 1998

HEATHER GRAHAM POZZESSERE

If looks could kill

Madison wasn't there when her mother was murdered, but she *saw* it happen. Years later, a killer is stalking women in Miami and Madison's nightmare visions have returned. Can FBI agent Kyle Montgomery catch the serial killer before Madison becomes his next victim?

"...an incredible storyteller!"—LA Daily News

1-55166-285-X
AVAILABLE FROM FEBRUARY 1998

MIRA®

JoAnn
ROSS

NO REGRETS

Three sisters torn apart by tragedy each choose a
different path—until fate and one man reunites them.
Only when tragedy strikes again can the surviving
sisters allow themselves to choose happiness—
if they dare pay the price.

"A steamy, fast-paced read."
—Publishers Weekly

MIRA®

1-55166-282-5
AVAILABLE FROM FEBRUARY 1998